Sarah Doudney

Godiva Durleigh

Vol. I

Sarah Doudney

Godiva Durleigh
Vol. I

ISBN/EAN: 9783337054199

Printed in Europe, USA, Canada, Australia, Japan

Cover: Foto ©Andreas Hilbeck / pixelio.de

More available books at **www.hansebooks.com**

GODIVA DURLEIGH.

A NOVEL FOR GIRLS.

BY

SARAH DOUDNEY,

AUTHOR OF
"A WOMAN'S GLORY," "WHERE THE DEW FALLS IN LONDON," ETC.

"Meanwhile to feel and suffer, work and wait,
Remains for us. The wrong indeed is great,
But love and patience conquer soon or late."
J. G. WHITTIER.

IN THREE VOLUMES.

VOL. I.

LONDON:
SAMPSON LOW, MARSTON & COMPANY
LIMITED.
St. Dunstan's House,
FETTER LANE, FLEET STREET, E.C.
1891.

TO

DOCTOR AND MRS. SYMES THOMPSON,

WITH GRATEFUL REMEMBRANCE

OF THEIR KINDNESS AND SYMPATHY

AND SINCERE APPRECIATION OF THEIR GOOD WORK,

I DEDICATE THIS BOOK.

CONTENTS OF VOL. I.

GODIVA DURLEIGH.

CHAPTER I.

HAUNTED BY A FACE.

" DON'T go indoors yet, father. Let us walk to the end of the street, close up to the old water-gate."

Morris Durleigh turned from the door and looked at his daughter for a moment. Her eyes met his with a frank, bright gaze, and then something which made you think of a ray of light passed over his face. It was a face that was visited now and then with a sudden illumination, but its habitual expression was thoughtful and sad.

"My good little girl," he said slowly and fondly. "Always contented with your surroundings — never pining to stretch your wings and fly away from this ugly old street!"

"Not ugly, father. Look at those soft shades of grey in the stone-work of Duke Steenie's old water-gate! And see how sunshiny the Embankment gardens are this morning! I like it all just as it is. Why should I want to fly away?"

It was a fine Sunday in February, and Buckingham Street seemed to be touched with the first sunbeams of Spring. Days of snow and bitter wind were yet to come, but here was a bright hour shining upon the London world after the gloom of a dark winter. Godiva Durleigh was a girl who always made much of her bright hours, and basked in the sunlight while it lasted.

"You must not abuse our street, father," she went on. "When I think of all the people who have lived here, I feel that they have left us a store of pleasant memories. My dear old gossip Pepys — my still dearer Dickens — and David Copperfield, in his 'young gentleman' days! They have never deserted their old haunts; I assure you that I am always exchanging friendly greetings with them."

"I have no time to spend with dream-companions, Godiva, although they are very good company:

'With live women and men to be found in the world—
Live with sorrow and sin—live with pain and with passion;'

to make my heart ache, and keep my brain busy, I lose my hold on the beings of yesterday."

"Dickens does not belong to yesterday, father," said the girl with soft enthusiasm. "He belongs to this time and all the coming times. A man who lives in the hearts of the people is always a man of to-day."

"Quite true, Godiva," Morris Durleigh answered, and the light passed over his face again.

They were standing at the end of the street looking through the iron railings at the water-gate. And presently Godiva saw that her father's eyes were gazing far away, over the gate across the gardens, into some invisible world beyond. She was familiar with this look of his, and always wondered what he was seeing. Sometimes he would answer the question which she seldom put in words; sometimes he kept silence.

After lingering for a few minutes, they

retraced their steps to their own door
again. They lived in apartments; the
parlour overlooking the street was the
room in which Morris Durleigh wrote his
leading articles, and did a great deal of
hard working and hard thinking undisturbed by the turmoil of London life.

After all, as Charles Kingsley said long
ago, there is no place so good to work
in as London. The small sounds that
would irritate us in the country silence
are swallowed up in the roar of the city.
And in Buckingham Street there was
really something like quietness; even
the piano-men had found out that they
gained nothing by grinding in front of
those dull-looking houses. Morris Durleigh's window was partially screened
from the gaze of the outer world by large
plants which were always in good con-
dition. In spite of the smoky atmo-

sphere they flourished bravely, and he liked to sit and write in the shade of their greenness.

Just before the door opened, Godiva asked some trifling question. But she received no reply, and one glance at Morris Durleigh convinced her that his mind was far away again. There was a look of trouble in his eyes which awakened her anxiety.

"Father," she said quickly, "there is something the matter, is there not? What is it?"

And as they crossed the threshold he answered in a reassuring tone—

"Nothing is amiss with me, Godiva. Only I am haunted by a face."

To a certain extent the answer was satisfactory. It was a relief to know that her father was neither ill nor threatened with any personal calamity.

As usual he had appropriated the trouble, real or imaginary, of some one else, and was groaning under the weight of another's burden. " To seek and to save "—to right the wrongs of the defenceless — to drag hidden cruelty into the strong light of day, and reveal it in all its hideousness—this was the work that he felt himself called to do, and he did it with all his might.

" He will tell me all about the face by-and-by," thought Godiva as she went flying upstairs to the top of the house. Her bedroom was under the roof, next door to Aunt Susanna ; and she would not, for the world, have exchanged places with the rich widow who was lodged lower down. She had learnt to love the room when she had first slept in it, a motherless child of ten, with Aunt Susanna watching over her slumbers.

And now another ten years had passed away, and she was a woman of twenty, looking back on the child's sorrow as a sad tale that is told; but the little room, with its simple comforts and decorations, was dear to her still.

She put off her jacket and bonnet and stood in front of the glass to smooth the soft rough hair, which took obstinate little twists and curls, and refused to submit to bondage. Godiva was seldom unnoticed, and yet you would have found it difficult to tell why she attracted your attention. The glass reflected a soft, pale, oval face, grey eyes with thick black eyebrows and lashes, and full lips that trembled at a word or a sound. But she was not thinking much of the face that she saw there; she was thoughtfully going over in her own mind the words that her father had spoken.

Would he suddenly announce his intention of starting off in search of the person he had seen? No matter how wild the quest appeared, she knew that he would go forth if the inner voice called him. The daughter never criticized the father's doings for a moment. She believed so implicitly in him and his mission, that nothing seemed too hard for him to accomplish. Even Aunt Susanna was silenced at once if she ventured to hint that Morris Durleigh was just a shade Quixotic.

Godiva ran downstairs,—a slim little figure flitting past the portly widow, who had just toiled heavily home from church. The stout woman looked after the girl with a passing feeling of envy, and then went back to her fireside chair, thanking her stars that she had a comfortable income without incumbrances. She had

always carefully avoided little Miss Durleigh, who was the daughter of a Com-
munist, or a Socialist, or a philanthropist;
she was quite sure about the termination
of the word, at any rate. Godiva, however, was utterly unconscious of the
widow's precautionary measures; but she
sometimes bestowed a pitying thought
on that poor Mrs. Naylor, who was
obliged to walk so slowly, and did not
care for books. The girl was so happy,
and so perfectly satisfied with her life,
that other lives seemed poor and tame
beside her own.

Morris Durleigh said little at luncheon,
and Aunt Susanna and Godiva talked
quietly between themselves. But afterwards, when he had gone to the easy-
chair in which he took his Sunday rest,
his daughter came to his side with a
gentle question.

"Father, are you still thinking about that face?"

"I wonder if I shall ever cease to think of it!" he said sadly. "It was a woman's face, Godiva. I saw her yesterday morning."

"Was she young, father? And where did you see her?"

"She was a mere girl. John Salterne had come to the office at one o'clock, and he dragged me out with him for a talk before luncheon. You know what a proser he is, Godiva. He started off on his favourite theme—this absurd philanthropy of mine, which is ruining my chance of success in life, and yours too."

"Never mind him, father."

"I wish I didn't mind him. If he were not such an honest man as he is, I shouldn't heed him at all. I can bear anything from a man I don't believe in.

But Salterne, with his exasperating dogmas and his detestable platitudes, is genuine to the core. It was while he was holding forth that I saw that poor girl. She was standing outside the railings in Savoy street, and looking at the old chapel and the garden."

"My dear chapel!" said Godiva softly. "It is a poem set in the middle of life's ugliest prose."

"That is just what the girl was thinking. Only her thoughts were sadder than yours have ever been. The little sanctuary, with its grass and trees, reminded her of some place that she had known and loved in happier days. Poor thing, she was over young to have had a past!"

"Was she pretty, father?"

"She ought to have been. God means all girls to be pretty and good, and they would be so if the wickedness of the world did not spoil them. Sin is always thwarting nature's intentions. I can picture that face in a moment of joy; it would then have been quite beautiful. But its look of hopelessness was beyond expression."

"Do you think she was very poor? Were her clothes in tatters?" asked Godiva, her grey eyes full of tears.

"No, she was decently dressed in a long tweed cloak. Salterne was holding me by the arm, and pouring his hoard of maxims into my ear. I wish I had stopped short and knocked him down! I wish I had done anything but what I did! The voice within me was louder than the nasal drawl of my dunderheaded old friend! And yet I let him drag me on."

Morris Durleigh sprang up suddenly from his chair, as if stung by the sharpness of an intolerable pain, and began to pace the room with rapid strides. Godiva went to him and put her arms within his.

"Dear father, you may see her another day," she said soothingly, although her tears fell fast.

"How can one tell? I refused to obey the voice, and it may not speak again. Even if I could rescue a thousand unhappy women I should never forget that one. A glimpse of the lost sheep was given me, but I did not lay hands on it and save it."

"But, father, are you sure that she was quite friendless? A little thing will sadden a girl sometimes, you know."

"Godiva, I have not studied human faces all my life without learning to read what is written on them. Some men spend their days in deciphering hiero-glyphics on rocks. As for me, I don't

care a straw about the history that a dead
and gone nation has left on stone. I go
about reading what sin and sorrow write
on flesh and blood ; my business is with
the living, and their life of to-day. If I
do not find that girl she may sink into
some unfathomable abyss. I tell you she
had come to the end of everything—love,
hope, the very means of existence. And
the memories that suddenly sprang up
round the little chapel were driving her
to despair ! Don't you know that the
sight of grey walls and green grass is more
than some hearts can endure ? "

He began to walk more slowly, and his
voice sank almost to a whisper.

" I will go to the street every day," he
said, after a pause. " She may be there
again."

CHAPTER II.

THE SALTERNES.

JOHN SALTERNE was a sober, plodding City man, with a slow brain and a kind heart. He spent a good many of his leisure moments in trying to pull Morris Durleigh into the beaten track, and never ceased to be astonished at the failure of his well-meant efforts. It was really quite true that Morris was doing hard work for small pay—quite true that he might have made a far better income if he had hearkened to the counsels of his old friend.

Honest John had done his best; he had heard with horror of Durleigh's resolution to give himself up to philanthropy, and when he found that Morris had helped to start a new Radical paper, his indignation knew no bounds. "The *Champion*," he said, "was the most abominable publication that had ever issued from the press. He could not hope that it would succeed, even for Morris's sake. The misguided man was deaf to all good, sensible, old-fashioned advice. He was living in a fever of wild hope and wilder effort, and by-and-by there would come the wretched consciousness of failure, and the final collapse. There was but one end for all these enthusiasts and dreamers."

Morris accepted these dismal predictions with perfect indifference. When John Salterne pressed him too hard, he would sometimes say that it was not for him to expect a better fate than his masters had had. "It is the seed that

lives and grows," he said, "not the hand
of the sower."   Nor did he despond when
the *Champion* proved unsuccessful.   He
went on with his work just the same,
doing editing and leader-writing with un-
flagging zeal.   It was his mission to speak
for the people, to put their wants into
words, to be their never silent voice.

"Oh, they are ready enough to speak
for themselves nowadays," Salterne remarked cynically.   "They don't ask you
to take the words out of their mouth."

It was very seldom that Morris resented
his old friend's plainness of speech.   John
Salterne was heavy and commonplace;
but a true man instinctively recognizes
truth, and John's steadfast integrity
atoned for his dulness.   In this case a
warm heart was held in bondage by dim
eyes and deaf ears.   He was not quick to
see misery, nor could he hear the endless

wail of suffering humanity. He was utterly unable to understand Morris, and yet he was capable of loving him well, and trying to serve him after his own fashion. Godiva, too, was second only to his own daughter, although he never ceased to find fault with her name.

But the girl rejoiced in being called after

"The woman of a thousand summers back,"

who had proved her love for the people of her town. In vain did John Salterne argue that the old story was merely an absurd fable; Godiva only pitied him for not realizing the golden truth that such a fable enshrined.

Once or twice a year Morris Durleigh and his daughter went to dine with the Salternes at their house at Notting Hill. They both dreaded these festivals, and returned gratefully to their ordinary life after having been feasted at the Salterne board.

If John was dull, Mrs. Salterne and Miss Salterne were hopelessly dense. They could not see anything to like or admire in the Durleighs, and always entertained them with great reluctance. But honest John was man enough to be master in his own house, and his wife and daughter were elaborately polite to poor Godiva. They could not help icing their smiles and words a little; it was so disagreeable to remember that Miss Durleigh's aunt was housekeeper in a lodging-house, and had been a second mother to her orphan niece. One could not expect much refinement in a girl who had been brought up under such circumstances. If Godiva innocently referred to Aunt Susanna they were always ominously silent.

Elizabeth Salterne talked persistently about the costumes worn at the drawing-rooms and fashionable weddings; and if Godiva tried to introduce the subject of art or literature she was sure to be coldly checked. Morris Durleigh was intimate with many men of mark; but Elizabeth refused to believe that his daughter had ever met any one who was worth knowing. She had no respect for the great thinkers of the day. The men who put their thoughts into pictures or poems were nobodies in Miss Salterne's estimation. Godiva used to resent this contemptuous indifference very bitterly sometimes, and it often cost her an effort to hide her feelings. She did not know that a time was coming when she should be thankful for this power of restraint, first exercised in John Salterne's house. The art of self-control (so much nobler than the art of self-defence) was destined to be constantly practised in her after-life.

It happened that the Durleighs were engaged to dine with the Salternes on Monday, a most unfortunate arrangement, for Morris and Godiva were both thinking of the unknown girl of Savoy Street, and the daughter was as much interested in her as the father. They had talked of her and thought of her till they could talk and think of nothing else. Godiva had a hopeful nature; already she had rehearsed a meeting with the stranger; already she had made up half-a-dozen histories of her, and every history had a happy ending. Before she went to bed she had opened her heart to Aunt Susanna.

Aunt Susanna Hayward understood her niece very well, and never chilled her

with an unsympathetic response, although
she sighed sometimes over the girl's
possible future. Godiva always followed
her father's lead with intense eagerness; she had the true spirit of an
enthusiast and partisan. There was no
room in her mind for the thousand and
one impulses and fancies which actuate
most young girls. All her interests were
absorbed in her father and his mission.
She was a great lover of books; but
her favourite authors were those who
wrote of men and women, and their
daily lives of struggle and strife, action
and rest. Her imagination was power-
ful and vivid, but it seldom carried her
out of the every-day world—that world
in which Morris Durleigh worked with
such unwearying zest.

"I wish we were not going to the
Salternes' to-morrow, aunty," she said,

with a deep sigh; "it's such a waste of time, you know. Their dinners always make us feel tired and depressed. Ten minutes of their society seem to weigh us down as no ten hours of our ordinary lives have ever done."

"But they mean to be kind to you," Aunt Susanna replied; "and I don't think they can help being dull."

Godiva was brushing out her curly brown hair for the night, and turned round, brush in hand, with rather a repentant look.

"Have I said anything ungrateful?" she asked. "Well, I will try with all my might to like them better. No, I can't! I can't like people in whom it is impossible to kindle any flame."

"I am afraid your father is all flame, Godiva. He is consuming himself."

She started, gave her thick hair a little

shake back, and fixed her clear grey eyes on Miss Hayward.

"That was said like Mr. Salterne, aunty, only you express yourself better than he does," she said rather coldly. "Of course father is consuming himself; he would tell you that he was created for no other purpose. But I think he will live quite as long as the Salternes, who do nothing but feed and pamper their bodies. I notice that there are all sorts of ailments peculiar to heavily selfish people."

"Now I have vexed you, my dear." Aunt Susanna was repentant in her turn. "Morris Durleigh is the grandest man I know. God bless him!"

Godiva instantly went towards her and kissed her.

Morris Durleigh went to his old friend's house with dreary resignation expressed in his voice and face. He always got on better with John when he was away from Notting Hill. Mr. Salterne at home was pompous and grandiose to the last degree. He treated Morris with good-natured indulgence, and spoke with such an air of patronage to Godiva that she lost sight of the real kindliness that lay hidden under the bombastic manner. The truth was that John tried on these occasions to put the Durleighs in a favourable light. He wanted the ladies of his house to see them to the best advantage. He endeavoured to throw all their peculi-arities into the shade, and the result of all these laudable efforts was the miserable depression of his guests.

The dinner passed off as usual. Morris talked little, and Godiva knew that con-versation was not required of her. She

was expected to listen meekly to the remarks made by the Salternes, and agree
with all they said. On the whole she
thought they were going on very well.
No one had touched on any unfortunate
subject; the talk had trickled monoton-
ously into safe channels, and she con-
gratulated herself on the prevailing tran-
quillity. But it is always unwise to shout
before you are out of the wood. A few
minutes later and Godiva's peace of mind
had taken flight.

They were all trifling over dessert, and
a momentary silence had fallen upon
them. Mrs. Salterne was the first to
break the pause; she addressed Godiva
with the affable little smile which she
always bestowed on her inferiors.

"You are happily spared any knowledge of domestic troubles, Miss Durleigh," she said. "Some friends of ours

have been shamefully robbed by a nurse-
maid.   I think you have heard me speak
of the Linghams, retired naval people,
very well connected?"

Godiva dropped a meek little "yes."

"Well, the captain spoils Mrs. Lingham entirely.   She is a great deal
younger than her husband; a delightful
person, but *so* unpractical.   I told her
from the first that she put too much confidence in her young nurse; but she said
that Joy had come to her with an excel-
lent character.   I believe the girl had
bewitched her."

"She was clever in managing children,"
remarked Elizabeth Salterne.   "And
Mrs. Lingham, poor thing, is not able
to cope with them at all.   So she was
compelled to leave them to Joy."

"I disapprove of lazy mothers," Mr.
Salterne put in.

"Oh, my dear, we mustn't be hard on delicate women," said his wife. "But let me finish my story. Poor dear Mrs. Lingham, in her trustful way, gave Joy a ten-pound note and sent her out shopping. While she was out, the Captain chanced to meet her, walking with a very fast-looking young man, and he came home and mentioned the circumstance. But his wife said at once that Joy had told her, from the first, that she was engaged to some one she had known from her childhood."

"The girl had always assumed an air of candour," said Elizabeth, with a cynical smile. "I used to think sometimes that she was almost too ingenuous!"

"By-and-by Joy returned," Mrs. Salterne continued. "But she had made no purchases. She came in, looking very strange and white, and said that

the ten-pound note was gone. Of course
the Linghams accused her at once of
walking with the young man, and she
admitted that she had met him. She
also admitted, after close questioning,
that she had given him her bag to hold
for a minute. The purse containing the
note was in the bag."

Morris Durleigh's interest was wide
awake. He had fixed his piercing blue
eyes on his hostess, and was waiting
impatiently to hear more.

"It's a marvel that she did return,"
said Elizabeth.

"I don't think so," Mrs. Salterne
replied. "She had lived with Mrs.
Lingham a year, and had quite succeeded
in winning her confidence. She thought
that her mistress would believe any im-
probable story that she chose to tell. But
my poor friend had opened her eyes at last."

"She opened them rather too late," said John Salterne.

"Well, my dear, I never thought that poor Mrs Lingham was keen - sighted. We are not all equally gifted. And then you know that the clergyman's letter of recommendation prepared her to trust in Joy. She was cruelly deceived."

"Who was the clergyman? Where did the girl come from?" inquired Morris Durleigh, with startling abruptness.

Mrs. Salterne tried to assume a dignified expression; she wished him to understand that she was accustomed to be deferentially addressed. But he did not care a pin about her dignity; he just wanted an answer to his question.

"Joy came from a remote village miles away," she said in measured tones. "She had lived with the vicar and his wife, and had taken charge of their child. Mother and child died, and then the vicar (I don't know his name), decided to go abroad. He saw Mrs. Lingham's advertisement, and instructed the girl to answer it; and he wrote a letter, as I have told you."

"And what has become of her now?"

Morris was more startling than ever, and the lady of the house was seriously displeased. Her eyes sought her husband, but he was dissecting the core of an apple, and did not meet her glance. Godiva looked anxiously at her father.

"I don't know," Mrs. Salterne answered curtly. "Of course the Linghams got rid of her at once. At the last she made a sensational scene, and offered to serve them without wages till she had paid back the ten pounds."

"They got rid of her at once," Morris

Durleigh repeated slowly. "And she was a country girl, without friends in London?"

"Oh, there was her young man, you know," said Elizabeth, with a sneer. "As to friends, Mr. Durleigh, I suppose she had quite a large circle. I dare say if she had kept her place she would have carried on an organized system of robberies with her associates."

"Isn't it possible to take a kinder view of her case?" asked Morris, fixing his piercing gaze on Elizabeth's face.

"Oh, you can take any view that pleases you," exclaimed Mrs. Salterne, reddening angrily, and rising. "We know that you always put on rose-coloured glasses when you look at the lower orders, Mr. Durleigh."

Elizabeth and Godiva rose also, the former flushed and scornful, the latter

pale and troubled. The door closed on
the ladies, and Morris Durleigh came
back to his seat, and prepared himself to
hear one of honest John's long lectures
on the folly of philanthropy.

But for once Mr. Salterne did not do
what was so confidently expected of him.
Even an elderly Pharisee devoted to
business pursuits and pompous respecta-
bility sometimes has a soft place in his
heart.

"It's very seldom that I concern myself about other people's servants," he
remarked, after a pause. "But it really
is a wonderful thing to see how hard some
women can be on a pretty girl. The
Linghams were always sending their nurse-
maid here with messages and parcels,
and that's how I got into the habit of
noticing her. My wife and daughter never
had a good word to say of the poor thing."

"John," said Morris suddenly, "did you observe a young woman in Savoy Street, on Saturday? She was looking through the railings into the Chapel garden. Just think a moment, will you?"

"My good fellow, no. That's just your way, Morris; instead of listening to me you were staring about, and trying to find out objects of charity."

"Her face struck me," said Durleigh, with a sigh. "I had a wild idea that she might have been the very girl you have been talking of."

"Nonsense," replied his host, with good-natured scorn. "A wild idea indeed! That nurse-maid girl must be gone back to the country."

CHAPTER III.

A JOYLESS JOY.

THE wind was as sharp as a needle, and now and then a snow-flake drifted down from the leaden skies. That one genial Sunday, with its sweet air and sunshine, had come like a delusive promise of better things, and even Joy Doveridge had been conscious that a faint ray of hope was stealing through the gloom of her life. But the light had faded, the dark, dreary winter had come back, and she was slowly treading that solitary and invisible path that leads to despair.

It seemed to her that years had gone

since she had been turned out of her place. She was a girl, with all a girl's fresh springs of vitality still bubbling up in her heart, and she was country-born and country-bred. The sight of a green meadow, a cluster of snowdrops in a cottage garden, or the clamour of rooks going home to roost in the tall elms, would have lifted her spirit out of the abyss of hopelessness into which it was sinking fast. But she had got none of these glimpses of her old home-life, and her heart within her was desolate.

It was bitterly cold, yet she stood close to the window, looking wearily across the Strand to the roofs of the opposite houses, now slightly sprinkled with snow. How miserable and sordid this London world seemed to her at this moment! She was alone, more utterly alone than she had ever been in her life, and sorrow and

anxiety had preyed upon her nerves and
undermined her health. She had been
feeling unlike herself for weeks; but to-
day there was something new in her
sensations that frightened her. Was she
going to be ill here? If she were ill she
might perhaps die, and be buried in some
crowded grave-yard in this cruel, noisy
London.

She would not have feared death if it
had come to her in her old country home.
There was a sweetness in the thought of
being laid down to sleep in the little
churchyard miles away. All her best
friends were slumbering there; her
grand-parents and the vicar's wife and
child had found a peaceful resting-place
under the fresh grass. And suddenly
the familiar scene rose up with vivid dis-
tinctness before her mental sight. She
saw it as it must be looking now in the

cloudy light of a February afternoon.
The trees that spread out their delicate
network of sprays against the grey sky,
and the little brown birds perched upon
the bare twigs ; the shiny green of the
ivy that mantled the old church walls ;
the quiet mounds where snowflakes and
snowdrops were lightly scattered together ;—in fancy she could see it all.

This was the picture that memory
showed her ; but what did she see with
her bodily eyes ? Houses blackened with
smoke and all the foul exhalations of a
great city, and down below " the raging,
brawling Strand." Hundreds of good
people were hurrying along in that endless procession—people who would have
spoken a kind word and done a charitable
deed if they had known that word and
deed were wanted. But Joy did not
know them, nor did they know her ; and

in her wretched mood the streets seemed to be thronged with restless, pitiless beings, all pursuing their own ends, all blind and deaf to any interests that did not concern themselves.

When the Linghams, in their wrath, had turned her out of their home at Notting Hill, the cook had taken a little pity on her at the last. She had hastily given Joy the address of an aunt of her's who took charge of a wine merchant's premises. Mrs. Bluff, cook had explained, was not a bad sort of woman, although she couldn't be expected to do a kindness for nothing. And poor Joy, confused, bewildered, crushed by the overwhelming suddenness of her misfortune, had gratefully accepted the bit of paper on which cook had scrawled a line to her relative.

The girl's sinking spirit had revived for an instant when she found that Mrs.

Bluff lived in the Strand. She knew that her George was lodging somewhere near the Strand; that was the address that she had put on the letters she had written to him. And she would seek him as soon as she could, and ask him to help her to find the lost money. George was so clever that he would be sure to think of some plan that had escaped her poor dazed brain.

A year had passed away since Joy had left her home in the country; but she had never once gone far from Notting Hill. When it was her turn to go out on Sunday afternoon George had met her, and had sometimes taken her for a long walk; but she had seen none of the sights of London. She was almost as much of a rustic now as she had been in the old days when she had picked the first primroses in the lanes. And George,

although he had often laughed at her
simplicity, had never even attempted to
give her a wider view of the world.

Her life in Captain Lingham's house
had been overcrowded with duties, and
she had enjoyed none of those sweet,
restful hours that she had known at the
vicarage. From morning till night she
had waited on her mistress and the children, doing a hundred things that Mrs.
Lingham's idle hands ought to have done.
There had been no order in the household; the little laws that a good mistress
makes were never put in force. Worst
of all, the housemaid had been bitterly
jealous of the pretty nurse, and had done
her many an ill turn without let or
hindrance. But Joy, saddened and
wearied as she often was, had kept up
her courage through everything, and had
tried hard to be contented with her lot.

Moreover, the house at Notting Hill was her only shelter from the rough blasts of the world. Joy was an orphan, left at five years old to the care of her mother's parents. They had brought the child up in their simple way in a poor village home, and she had gone to the vicarage as soon as she was old enough to take a situation. And then for five happy years she had served those who were themselves " serving," in singleness of heart, fearing God.

It was very easy to be good at the vicarage—so easy that a bad girl would have lacked opportunities of being bad. The sweet, untempted life glided on as if it would never come to an end. But a woman is seldom destined to spend all her days in a " garden enclosed; " and even Joy Doveridge sometimes had vague thoughts about the world outside of her walls of peace.

Her first sharp sorrow was the death of the little child; and although others had noticed the fast-declining strength of the vicar's wife, Joy's inexperienced eyes failed to detect the signs of decay. She thought that Mrs. Elmslie was worn with grieving for her little son, and never dreamt that her dear mistress was so soon to be laid to rest by her boy's side. But the end came rapidly; and then Joy knew that the rose-covered walls that had sheltered her life were broken down at last. She was now to see what kind of country lay outside of the vicarage garden, and she must learn to do her part in a wider sphere.

When Mr. Elmslie had advised her to go to the Linghams he believed that she would find a safe home with them. Some people whom he knew had spoken in the highest terms of Captain Lingham's wife.

And it was true that Joy's new mistress
was soft and sweet on the surface; you
might have thought her tender all
through, if you had not chanced to go
too deep, and touch upon the hard core
of her selfishness. She loaded Joy's back
with burdens which a more experienced
girl would have utterly refused to carry;
and she never gave a single thought to
her young nurse's inner life.

Joy Doveridge and George Hunter had
been sweethearts ever since they could
remember. He was a workhouse boy,
whose parents were unknown; she belonged to the poorest people in the
village. Together they had sat on a stile
to scare the crows, sharing their scanty
meal, and howling at the birds between
mouthfuls. Together they had gone
blackberrying in the copse, and brought
back a well-filled basket between them,

coming down the village hill like Jack and Jill, and earning many a penny as the fruit of their joint labour. Very early in their lives they had entered into partnership, and when they grew old enough to "keep company," the vicar himself gave his sanction to the engagement.

In those golden days, away in the little Hampshire village, life was giving many of its best gifts to the boy and girl, although they knew it not. It was a bliss to live and dream away a bright hour under the hedge, while the honeysuckle hung its trailers above their heads, and the wheat-ears nodded in the warm breath of the summer wind. But not until long afterwards did George or Joy realize that this was the sweetest part of their lives. They thought that it was only the prelude to a lovely song which the future was to sing.

George Hunter was a slim, well-made youth, looking younger than he really was. He had rather a gipsy face, with dark eyes, and dark hair which curled close to his head. His rise in the world was rapid; from crow-scarer he became a stable-helper in the village doctor's establishment; and then a friend of the doctor's, who had come down from town, took handy George back with him to London.

"He is getting on *so* well," said Mrs. Elmslie to her husband, after reading one of George's letters to his betrothed. "I shouldn't wonder if he were to come back here, and want to settle, and then we should lose our Joy."

George had been away nearly two years when the vicarage household was suddenly broken up. And poor Joy, in spite of grief and loneliness, was not afraid to go to London. He was there, and perhaps it would not be long before the much-talked-of little home would be ready for habitation. He was so clever, and he knew how to do so many things, that he was sure to make money.

George was really glad to have his sweetheart in town ; but they did not meet oftener than once a fortnight. Followers were not allowed indoors, and Joy could not go out every Sunday. Sometimes she complained to her lover of Mrs. Lingham's unreasonable demands; but, although George always sympathized, he did not say anything definite about the future. He spoke hopefully, almost enthusiastically, of his prospects, but they seemed to be enshrouded in a glorious haze. Perhaps it was because he was so clever that he had been " all things by turns, and nothing long." Anyhow, he had a way of jumping into situations and out of them with a rapidity which astonished the simple-minded Joy.

"I will go over it all again," the girl thought. "I will begin at the beginning of that dreadful afternoon when the purse was lost. I must keep on thinking, and thinking, and thinking; and then, perhaps, something fresh will come into my mind."

And she did go over it all again. She remembered that it was a bitter January afternoon, and the clock was striking the quarter after two when she entered the nursery in her plain hat and cloak, ready for her wintry walk.

Mrs. Lingham was in a very good humour that day; a new dress had just been sent home, and fitted her perfectly; her husband had promised her a sealskin jacket, and an admiral, living in Mayfair, had invited them to dinner. She was a pretty, cosy-looking little woman ; and as she sat in the arm-chair by the nursery fire, with the children round her, she seemed to be a complete impersonation of home peace. The comfortable room, with a great rocking-horse prancing in one corner, and a doll's house in another, was a cheerful refuge on a bleak, windy day.

The seven little ones were already devising plans for their afternoon's amusement, and Emily, the tall housemaid, was taking all the lesson-books and picture-books down from the book-case, and putting them in order—a task which she performed without much good-will. "It was hard that she should be set to do the nurse's work," she had said, in a grumbling tone, which was meant to reach Joy's ears. Joy, however, was getting used to Emily's unpleasant remarks, and paid but little heed to them.

Close to Mrs. Lingham's elbow was the small round table, laden with Joy's work-box and a pile of hose to be mended. The nurse's little hand-bag was lying on the top of the box. This bag, of dark-green morocco, had been given to Joy by her mistress as a Christmas gift, and was highly prized by its owner; first, because it was the only thing that Mrs. Lingham had ever given her, and, secondly, because, being a country-girl, any tasteful knickknack had a great charm in her eyes. When Joy entered, Mrs. Lingham took up the bag, and drew her purse out of her pocket.

"See, Joy," she said, "I am going to trust you with my purse, and a ten-pound note in it. Here is the note; you must be very careful in counting the change."

She opened the purse, showed Joy the little piece of flimsy paper, closed the snap again, and put it into the hand-bag.

"I'll be very careful, ma'am," the girl replied.

"You have your list, and know exactly what to buy," Mrs. Lingham went on. "But, oh, I was forgetting something! I want some new strings for my bonnet. Joy, you must go and take the bonnet out of the wardrobe, and cut a little bit off one of the strings. Remember that the new ribbon must match the old strings perfectly. Be very particular, and make haste, or all the daylight will be gone."

Joy ran off at once to her mistress's bedroom, and looked into the wardrobe for the bonnet. But it was not there; and it was very seldom indeed that any of Mrs. Lingham's belongings were ever found where they were supposed to be. Her faithful maid at last discovered the bonnet in one of the cupboards. She cut off a bit of the ribbon, and pinned it securely on the front of her cloak, that it might not be lost.

When she went back to the nursery she found Mrs. Lingham settled in a luxurious attitude of repose. The easy-chair was pulled to the front of the fire, and her mistress, with her feet on the high fender, was lounging in it with an open book. She was too lazy and comfortable even to turn her head when Joy entered.

"Don't forget your bag," she said, in a drowsy voice. "And don't dawdle, or lose anything."

"I will be very careful, ma'am," the girl repeated.

The lady said no more, and Joy took

her bag from the round table. It was clear that Mrs. Lingham did not mean to do any mending that afternoon, although she had talked about it. She had deliberately turned her back upon the little work-table and the pile of hose, and was basking in' the glow of the fire. The children were all grovelling on the floor upon hands and knees, absorbed in the arrangement of an extensive zoological garden. Joy was young enough to feel that she would have liked to have set up the impossible trees, and placed the ferocious animals in their red and yellow dens; but she had to go her way, out into the cold. Emily, the housemaid, was still sulkily dusting the books, and taking no notice of anything.

It was bleak and bitter out of doors, and very few people cared to brave the cutting north-easter that stripped the

suburban trees of their last dry leaves. Joy
hurried on, impatient to accomplish her
business, and return to the warm nursery.
But just as she was drawing near Notting
Hill Gate, her heart gave a quick throb of
delight. There was George—her own
George—walking with his shoulders up to
his ears, and his hands in his pockets;
but her pleasure changed swiftly to
anxiety at the sight of his haggard face.

"It's very nice to meet you, dear," she
said, as he turned to walk by her side.
"But is anything the matter?"

"Not much," he answered. "I'm a
little out of sorts, that's all. What brings
you out on such a day as this, Joy?"

She told him, readily enough, about the
shopping that she had to do, and added
that her mistress had been kinder of late,
and had seemed to set a higher value on
her willing service. George listened with

his outward ears; but it was plain that his thoughts were wandering. The wind whistled round them dismally, and he shivered and pulled up his coat-collar.

Joy stopped so suddenly that he started. Her boot-lace was untied, and there was nothing for it but to pause, and put her foot upon a convenient door-step.

"Let me tie the lace for you," said her lover dreamily.

"No, thank you, George; I can do it more quickly," she replied. "But please hold my bag. And, oh, do be careful, for there's a ten-pound note in mistress's purse inside it!"

She wore stout country boots, with thick laces, and the tying was a work of some seconds. It was done at last, and she turned round to take the bag from George's hand.

At that moment something in her

lover's expression gave her a shock, and then came a sinking of the heart utterly beyond her small power of analyzation. All her foregone beliefs seemed to be revolutionized in that brief instant. She had been so perfectly convinced of her complete knowledge of George,—she had believed herself so thoroughly acquainted with his very thoughts,—that this new look of his was chilling her with an indescribable fear. Never before had he seemed so like a stranger, living a life entirely apart from her own. What dreadful secret was he hiding from the faithful little soul who had been comrade and friend as well as sweetheart? In the old Hampshire days there had been but one heart and one mind between them.

"I don't think you are well, George," she said, in a faltering voice.

"Indeed I am." The answer came

slowly, and with a visible effort. "That is, as well as any one can be in such unbearable weather. But, Joy, I came here to meet a man who hasn't turned up, and now I must hurry off to the City. You are going into this shop? Well, good-bye, dear; I am glad to have seen you."

They parted at a linen-draper's door, and Joy looked wistfully into George's face; but the dark eyes avoided meeting hers. In another second he was out of sight; he seemed to vanish, somehow; and the girl bethought her of all the purchases that she had to make.

She tried to put George out of her mind when she stood before the counter with her list in her hand. But it was remembered against her afterwards that she forgot the bonnet ribbon, and while yards and yards of flannel and calico were

measured off, her thoughts went straying
after her lover.

"And the next thing, madam?" said
the civil shopman, who "madamed"
every woman, rich or poor, gentle or
simple. He had to repeat his question
before Joy heard and answered him.

"Nothing more," she replied. "I will
pay you for the things at once."

The bill was made out and handed to
her, and she mechanically opened her
little bag. Some seconds passed, and she
still stood staring into the bag with a
bewildered look on her face.

"The purse is gone," she said at last,
her blue eyes wide open, and all the rose-
colour dying out of her cheeks.

The shopman knew her by sight, and
administered ready consolation. "Not
the slightest doubt that the purse was
left at home," he said; "such things were

happening every day; there really was no need for any anxiety." But poor Joy's troubled heart could not accept this comfort. She had seen, with her own eyes, that the note was put into the purse, and the purse into the bag; and she set off homeward at a flying pace, her face as white as death, and her brain in a whirl.

The storm which broke upon her defenceless head had left traces which no after-peace could ever entirely remove. They would not listen to any of the timid words she uttered; they could not see that, frightened and miserable as she was, she yet concealed nothing, but frankly admitted that she had met and walked with her lover; and they sneered at her eager promises to make good their loss. Captain Lingham's wrath burnt all the more fiercely because his wife had neglected to take the number of the note.

Mrs. Lingham, who beheld her hope of a sealskin vanishing like smoke, was transported with rage. And at last it seemed to Joy that she was swept out of the house in a whirlwind of hysterical screams, threats, and reproaches. The children stood looking on at the scene with round eyes and scared faces, and not one of the little voices dared to whisper a good-bye.

In the midst of all this turmoil and misery, her bewildered mind took hold of one thought, and clung to it as a drowning man clings to a spar. She would go to George's lodging, and ask him to help her. George was not dull and slow like some of the good folks down in the old village; he had always been sharper than any one else, quicker in seeing his way through a difficulty, readier in finding an answer to a puzzling question. If any

one on earth could clear up this dreadful
mystery it must be George.

Alas! she was here, at the end of her
scanty resources, brought to bay with
fortune in a dreary London lodging. And
George was gone. She had failed to find
him, or any trace of him. The people in
his lodging-house had told her that he
had gone away : and that was all.

Slowly, and not until she had put it
from her passionately, thousands of times,
the deadly belief had forced its way into
her mind at last. It was her lover who
had stolen the money. "Handy George,"
who had always been so nimble and
clever with his fingers, had taken the
purse out of the bag while her back was
turned towards him.

She remembered that her old grand-
mother had said that George looked as
if he had gipsy blood in his veins. No

one had known the boy's parents; no
one could say whether he came of the
wandering race or not. In her earlier
days Joy had never thought anything
about George's origin; but now that she
was tormented with doubts and fears,
certain vague rumours came drifting
back.

If she could only have believed in him
still, she might possibly have plucked up
heart to battle with misfortune. If she
could have found herself once more in
her little room at the vicarage, looking
out upon the sycamore that brushed the
pane—if she could have seen the early
death of the day behind the dear old
hills, and the last silver lights in the
wintry west—ah, then her childhood's
faith in her lover might have revived.
But what hope could visit her in this
dark chamber, with its dirty paint and

stained wall-paper, and its two broken-backed chairs? And what whisper of comfort could be heard while this hoarse roar came up from the crowded thorough-fare below? She seemed to see her life laid bare before her eyes—her poor hope-less life—not as she had always imagined it would be, but as it really was.

Godiva Durleigh would never have been thoroughly miserable as long as London sights and sounds were near. The ceaseless roar of the Strand was music in her ears; the hurrying throngs of men and women were brothers and sisters, children of one Father, knit to-gether by common sorrows and common delights. The daughter of the philan-thropist felt her heart beating freely when its beats were echoed by the throb-bings of other hearts. In a crowd she was never lonely, because humanity, even when degraded and debased, touched a sympathetic cord within her. Godiva, like Joy, had an infinite capacity for suffering; but the balm for her wounds did not grow in solitary places; it was watered by the tears of a crowd.

Poor Joy was too timid and too little accustomed to city life to gain courage as days went on. Servants were wanted, it was true; but what safe home would open its doors to a girl without references? At first she had hoped that she could obtain a place by simply saying that she was willing to work; and, in her ignorance of the world, had looked forward to honest service with a faint sense of comfort. But disappointment met her at every turn.

CHAPTER IV.

A DREAM.

THERE was neither help nor encouragement to be had from Joy's landlady. Mrs. Bluff had thought slightingly of her lodger from the first moment of her arrival, and had not scrupled to speak her mind.

"You ain't the sort of gal to make your way up here," she had remarked more than once. "There hisn't a particle of brass in you, and brass is more wanted than anything else, and fetches the best price in the market. Why don't you go back to the country?"

" There's no one to go back to," Joy
would answer sadly. "All my friends
are dead. And my village is such a
small place, that very few servants are
wanted there."

Out of doors it was growing darker
and darker, and Joy began to realize
that her limbs were stiff with cold. A
light suddenly appeared in the attic
window of the opposite house, and the
girl vaguely wondered whether there was
any heart there as heavy as her own.

This was Friday, to-morrow she must
pay the weekly sum agreed upon for
board and lodging. And then? Well,
then her means would be quite exhausted. She cast a glance towards
the box that she had brought with her,
and began, with a weary brain, to
reckon up what its simple contents
were worth. She had some decent

clothes, made in plain, country fashion, of good materials.   Mr. Elmslie had behaved thoughtfully and generously, and supplied her with an ample outfit. It would be bitter, indeed, to part with those neat garments for half or quarter of their value; and yet they were the last frail barrier between herself and beggary.

Shivering, and feeling wretchedly ill, she crept down flight after flight of steep stairs to the kitchen, where Mrs. Bluff always took her meals.   The woman was sitting by a blazing fire, toasting a muffin, and there was something in the aspect of her coarse face that made Joy take a seat as far away from her as she could.

Mrs. Bluff was not absolutely drunk, but she had been drinking enough to bring all her worst qualities into play.

She fixed a hard scrutinizing gaze on Joy's wan cheeks and lustreless eyes. There were a loaf and butter and tea-pot on the table, and the girl half timidly poured out a cup of tea.

"You're looking mortal bad," said Mrs. Bluff, with brutal candour. "T'wont be long afore you're laid up, and it don't answer my purpose to have sick people 'ere, I can tell you."

"I hope I'm not going to be ill," Joy answered, trying to steady the hand that held the cup.

"There's no good in 'opin' about a thing wot's certain to come to pass," Mrs. Bluff said, in an oracular tone. "I ain't often deceived, and I always told yer that yer wouldn't do for London life. My niece, as was a fool to send yer 'ere, must have knowed it too. Now what I want to know is—

when are yer going to clear out o' this ? "

Joy felt herself beginning to tremble from head to foot, and for some seconds she could not think of any words to speak. Had Mrs. Bluff divined that her little stock of money was exhausted ? Partly ; but the woman had a chance of letting Joy's bedroom to a young man, and she was tired of the girl's sad face and silent ways—tired, too, of the restraint which a pure nature unconsciously imposes on the grovelling souls around it. When Joy was near she sometimes found herself using choicer language than usual, and walking a little more circumspectly than she would have done if her quiet lodger had been far away.

"I thought that perhaps you would be good enough to keep me a little longer," said the girl, in a faltering voice. " I meant to tell you that when I have paid you to-morrow I shall only have one shilling left. But if you would look over my clothes—— "

" There, do shut up, for goodness' sake ! " Mrs. Bluff's face expressed un-mitigated disgust. " Whatever do you spose I could do with your country-cut things ? No, no, this ain't an old clo' shop. You'll jest make up yer mind to be off arter you've paid me. And you may leave yer box here till six o'clock to-morrow night, and not a minute later, so 'elp me."

When Mrs. Bluff said " so 'elp me," she brought her hard fist down on the deal table with a bang that set the cups and saucers rattling. Joy did not attempt to move her by any further appeal; there was nothing in her to respond to a prayer, no soft place in her flinty heart that could be touched with a cry of distress. One glance at her face, and Joy's lips were sealed.

The girl's silence irritated Mrs. Bluff, who was in the mood when anything in the shape of a scene is welcome. Finding that Joy did not speak, she presently began a series of insulting remarks about young women with no characters a-coming into decent 'ouses and expecting to take root in 'em. Sich conduct was not what Eliza Bluff could put up with. To be eaten out of 'ouse and 'ome by people without references, and nothing but a trumpery box of country-cut cloes, was anything but what Eliza Bluff considered right. Honest widders, like Eliza, had theirselves to purwide for, and couldn't be filling idle mouths as 'ad no claim on 'em.

Joy bore it all patiently, until the " honest widder's " voice began to rise higher and higher, and her face grew redder and redder. Then, with a soft step, the girl crept away, and climbed the steep stairs to her wretched bed-room. When she had bolted herself in, she knelt down by the window, and tried to say some of the old prayers that she had learnt in her earliest years; but she was faint and cold, and could not collect her thoughts. There was nothing for it but to put out the light, and go shivering and restless to her pillow.

At last, after weary hours of wakeful-ness, a deep slumber did for a time over-take her, and she dreamed a dream. The brief sleep that came to Joy after mid-night was very sweet. She had not known such a quiet rest for many weeks.

She dreamt that she was toiling slowly.

up the narrow lane that led to the grey church at home; and although there were no leaves on the trees, and no flowers in the hedges, the birds were singing clear and strong. She listened to the bird-notes with an indescribable, ecstatic gladness; dead feelings seemed to wake up again; her old faith in God was coming back. At the summit of the hill the lane widened; there were the red walls of the vicarage garden, and here was the open gate of the quiet churchyard. By that gate she took her stand, and waited for some one who would, she knew, be sure to come. This waiting lasted—who shall say how long? She could not herself have told, when, long afterwards, she looked back upon the dream.

The place was quite unchanged. She stood looking at the gravelled path that

led straight to the Gothic portal, and
the green mounds rising on each side of
the way. It was fresh and still and
peaceful here; the winter was scarcely
over yet, but all dread of storm and
wind was gone. Something that breathed
faintly of hope—some subtle hint of
Easter joy—was in the very air. She
did not find the time long, but she was
conscious of continued expectation; and
at last the one for whom she waited
came, and stood before her face to
face.

It was her dear mistress, Mrs. Elmslie,
who had come to her, not dressed in any
unfamiliar fashion, but wearing her old
grey gown, and smiling the old placid
smile, which had always set Joy's heart
at rest. If she had appeared in a white
robe, holding a palm-branch in her hand,
the girl would have missed this sweet

sense of familiarity which made the meeting seem a natural and simple thing.
Even in her dream she knew that the
vicar's wife was no longer numbered
among the living; yet she did not feel
that her return to every-day life was
strange.

And then in the twinkling of an eye the
scene changed. The wide, open country
and the hills were gone; there was only a
little space of grass and wintry trees; and
a church, greyer, older, and smaller than
the village church, appeared before her
eyes. The roar of London sounded in
her ears again; the uncertain life with
its burdens of fear and sorrow had come
back. But somehow the load was easier
to bear. She looked up at her mistress
and saw that her face was very calm
and sweet; and the well-known voice
spoke to her in a quiet tone.

" You have been here before, Joy," it said ; " and you must come here again."

She woke up, and found the daylight stealing slowly into the room ; and then she rose, shook off sleep, and looked out upon the grimy fronts of the opposite houses. It was not snowing now ; there were even vague promises of sunshine. She had slept later than usual, and her sickening dread of Mrs. Bluff's temper revived as she went wearily downstairs.

But, for some unexplained cause, Mrs. Bluff was not disposed to be quarrelsome this morning. She received Joy's little pile of silver with civility, and then suddenly assumed a melancholy air, and sighed loudly over the badness of the times. Joy swallowed a few mouthfuls of bread, and drank some tea, even venturing to warm herself by the fire, before she went upstairs to pack her box.

When she had closed the lid of her trunk she put on her bonnet and cloak, and wondered vaguely where she should be when night came round again? She was growing almost apathetic now, and even the sight of her bloodless face and dull eyes reflected in the glass, did not greatly move her. She had been a pretty girl once—not long ago—but what good was in her youth and beauty? What interest had she in her hair and dress, or in anything? A girl who has lost the innocent vanities of girlhood has lost hope in life.

George was lost to her for ever; but she was too dull and spiritless to realize that loss. She only felt vaguely that all her future had been swept away, and that nothing remained but this grim inexorable present with its threats of homelessness and starvation. Without hope and with-

out energy she left the dreary room, and
went downstairs out into the street.

Her heart ached under a heavy load of
pain, and the roar of the Strand was
almost more than her over-strained nerves
could bear. Oh, to see once more that
beloved friend who had come to her in
last night's dream! Oh, to be taken
gently by the hand, and led out of this
turmoil to some peaceful spot where there
was rest!

With an intense longing came a swift
remembrance of the dream-voice, and the
words that it had seemed to speak:—"You
have been here before, Joy; and you
must come here again." She must go
and look at the small grey church, standing in the grassy garden where there
were old tombstones and ivy and trees.
The sight of it might do her a little good,
for it would bring the dream nearer to

reality. It was not so very much unlike the old church at home; and it might be possible to call up a vision of Mrs. Elmslie, looking just as she had looked in the dream. There was so little comfort in this noisy every-day world that it was not strange if a sick soul sought solace in a realm of phantoms.

Her pale forlorn face met with scanty notice in the Strand, and if she was intentionally pushed or stared at, she was too weary to resent a rudeness. The clocks were striking twelve as she turned down the sharp slope of Savoy Street; there were gleams of sunshine; and a group of choir-boys was standing outside the iron railings that protected the Chapel garden. Joy did not even glance at the boys, and they did not seem to observe her as she stood leaning against the gate.

What was the girl thinking of, as she

stood there, holding the railings with a tight clasp? Of old peaceful Sundays long past; of dear ones who had gone on before her to the great resting-place of love; of a time of peace and re-union which might even now be drawing very near. She did not care to leave this spot. It did not matter to her, just then, that the day was slipping by, and she had not yet found a place of shelter for the night.

When a hand lightly touched her shoulder it scarcely startled her. Perhaps she had expected something; perhaps her dream had left so vivid an impression on her brain that she was half prepared for an event. A man with a grave gentle face, was looking at her searchingly and kindly; and he spoke to her in words that she remembered long afterwards. "You were here last Saturday. And I have come every day to look for you."

This was strange indeed. But when Joy met the gaze of those mild, yet penetrating blue eyes, she thought of a picture of the Good Shepherd which had hung in the nursery at the vicarage. Later on, when she had learnt more of the world, and of those who are doing good in it, she knew that there is a *seeking* look on the faces of the Good Shepherd's followers; a look which great artists know well, and have stamped on their ideal saviours of men. Morris Durleigh's eyes always told the story of his life and the desire of his life.

" I want to know all about you," he went on quietly. " What is your name ? I think you have come from the country."

" My name is Joy Doveridge, sir, and I am country-born," the girl answered simply.

Her voice was husky and weak, but

Morris could tell that it was naturally
sweet; and the poor wan face was flush-
ing faintly as hope began to stir again in
her heart. In spite of all John Salterne's
good-natured scorn, his instinct had been
true. It was indeed the friendless country-
girl whom he had so eagerly sought and
found.

"I have heard your story," he said,
"and I see how it is with you now. You
have not found another place?"

"No, sir." Her lips quivered. "If
you have heard everything, you know
that I was sent away in disgrace from
Captain Lingham's house. It seemed to
them that I'd stolen the note and given it
to the young man I was engaged to.
Nothing will ever make them believe
that I am innocent. But God knows,
sir, that I am willing to work night and
day till I've paid back the money! It's

ten pounds, sir, that's gone; and it might take a long time to earn as much, but I'll do it if I only get a chance."

"You shall have the chance." Morris spoke in a firm, steady tone, which carried certainty into her mind at once. "But you are looking white and ill, and it is not good for you to stand here in the cold. Did you come because this place reminded you of some country church far away?"

"Yes, sir; and partly because I was dreaming of it last night," said Joy, drawing a deep breath of relief, and letting go her convulsive hold of the railings. Her fingers were aching and stiff, and she did not know how long she had been clinging to those railings before her new friend had found her. The sun was shining brightly now, striking on the drops of moisture that clung to the boughs of the plane-trees until they glittered like gems. There were sparks of light flashing here and there in the old chapel garden ; sparrows were flying about the rugged grey walls. Was this the beginning of spring ?

Joy asked no questions when they moved away from the chapel ; she walked quietly by her conductor's side, quite satisfied in trusting herself to his guidance. As they went along he inquired if she had anything belonging to her, and she told him, in a few words, about Mrs. Bluff, and the box that was left in her care. Then they turned into Buckingham Street, and stopped before the house which had the tall green plants in the parlour window. Her senses were getting quicker now, for she fancied she saw a young face behind the screen of leaves.

Morris Durleigh had taken out a latch-key, but before he could use it the house door was thrown open, and a girl met them on the threshold. Joy looked up at her, and the memory of Godiva, seen as she was at that instant, was imprinted for ever on the tired woman's heart and brain.

It was one of Godiva's moments of illumination. She had utterly forgotten self; and her face was lit up by the beautiful eager spirit that flamed within her. Her countenance, with its soft innocent lips and clear eyes, was a model of tender womanhood. She held out a slender hand to Joy, and drew her gently into the house.

" Ah, you have found her, father," she cried. " Something told me that you would not fail."

" Something told me so too," he answered, with a peaceful smile. " Godiva, this is Joy Doveridge ; we have heard her

story from the Salternes, and there is no
need to ask her many questions. We
must find her first a resting-place, and
then a working-place."

It was no small surprise to Mrs. Bluff
when a gentleman asked to see her, and
requested that Joy Doveridge's box might
be brought downstairs. The "honest
widder" began to wish that she had
been less hasty in parting with her young
lodger. There was an air of refinement
about Joy which had puzzled Mrs. Bluff,
while it had irritated her. It was clear,
even to her coarse mind, that the girl had
been well brought up, and had lived with
people of no inferior degree. And now it
appeared to her that some of those people
had discovered Joy, and were about to take
her under their protection again. But
nothing was to be extracted from the
gentleman who came for the box, and

Mrs. Bluff expended all her best blandishments upon him in vain.

And so Joy passed away out of the noisy house in the Strand, and left not a trace behind her.

CHAPTER V.

SUNSHINE AND CALM.

THERE was an old-fashioned house at Richmond, with a garden sloping down to the river, which the Durleighs loved to visit. It was not a large house, but it had a certain dignity which belongs to substantial red bricks, mellowed and darkened by time, and ivy that has taken years to grow. No one had thought it worth while to take out the old many-paned windows, and replace them with modern bays; and no one had felt it necessary to widen the front door, which was very narrow, and was surmounted by an arch filled in with glass. The people who lived there were not fond of alterations, and steadily objected to the intrusion of carpenters and masons. When you had passed through the narrow door, you found yourself confronted by a narrow staircase, and received a general impression of dimness and primness. Of course such a house was clearly meant to be inhabited by two old maids, and a quiet pair of elderly women had dwelt in it for many a year.

They were *real* old maids, who never dreamt of dressing up to the fashion, or of changing any of "their ways" because those ways were somewhat out of date. They wore their soft white hair in barrel curls, kept in place by the tortoiseshell combs which had been given to them when they were little girls, and pinned their laces with the memorial brooches that they had had in their teens. They never seemed to have lost any of those quaint little gold and silver and coral links, which connected them with their girl-hood; everything had been religiously preserved, and was brought into common use. Godiva Durleigh used to think that they never broke anything in that house, nor threw it away.

Yes; they had kept everything. Even their valentines were to be found pasted into albums and scrap-books, and they had a thick volume of beautifully copied music. Upstairs in a wardrobe there were two wax dolls, of a ghastly pallor, dressed in the garb of little girls of sixty years ago. As to needlework, they had enough to supply an exhibition, and their drawing-room was quite a garden of Berlin-wool flowers. But although they surrounded themselves with these relics of their past life, they did not shut the present out of their hearts. No one, save Morris Durleigh, perhaps, knew how large a portion of their income was spent upon those who were " desolate and oppressed " in the noisy overcrowded world of to-day.

Henrietta Kemple was two years older than her sister Charlotte, and had the aspect of an elderly dove. Pretty, even in age, with small, regular features and mild eyes, her appearance soothed you even before she opened her lips to say pleasant things. Her grey gown fitted her plump figure perfectly; and in winter she wore a dainty cross-over of Chinese silk, pinned on her bosom with a little pearl brooch. Godiva liked to watch her delicate hands, always in mittens, moving over her work, and was pleased with the lavender scent that clung to the grey gown. Miss Kemple's old age was a beautiful and imperceptible decay. She had no bitter regrets, no corroding doubts and cares, and these last years were as peaceful as a summer twilight. Life's colours were dimmed; its gay bird-voices had died away; but even the slowly-creeping darkness was full of holy promises, and sweet whispers of an eternal dawn.

If Henrietta made one think of a dove, there was certainly a good deal of the sparrow about Charlotte. She was small and spare, and her movements were like hops and pecks; her favourite colour was brown, and her eyes were those keen twinkling hazel eyes which keep their youthful brightness a long while. Never as pretty as her sister, she was sharper and wittier than Henrietta had ever been. Naturally, she was disposed to take a cynical view of life, such as might be

expected of one who had a keener obser-
vation for people's sins than for their
virtues. But Henrietta was always near
to make excuses for the sinners, and a
soft word or two from her never failed to
silence Charlotte's sharp tongue.

The sisters loved each other so dearly
that their dissimilar characters were in
perfect harmony. Charlotte knew how
much she owed to Henrietta's restraining
gentleness, and Henrietta never ceased to
admire Charlotte's practical cleverness
and energy. Long years ago, in their
girlhood, they had had those little quarrels
which arise out of high spirits and clashing wills. But they never quarrelled
nowadays, partly because all their apples
of discord had vanished, but chiefly
because their life was so sweet and calm,
that they could not bear to destroy the
peace or mar the melody.

They kept two servants. Cook, a strong, brown-faced woman with sad eyes, had lived with them for twenty years. Her husband, a burglar, had been convicted of manslaughter and sentenced to penal servitude for life. The Kemples had taken compassion on the miserable wife, and had received her into their house at the risk (their friends said) of having their throats cut, and their plate stolen. But cook neither drank nor stole, nor held any communication with doubtful characters. During all those long years she had never gone beyond the garden on week days, and the church on Sundays. And so it came to pass at length that her story was forgotten by all save her mistresses and herself.

Housemaids came, got on very well with the grave, silent woman in the kitchen, stayed a year or two, and then married. But the latest comer, although she was prettier than any of her predecessors, seemed utterly indifferent to the attentions of the butcher and the baker. She was never known to linger at the door when the tradespeople's young men brought parcels, and she never asked for a Sunday out, or an evening to go to see her friends. They called her Joy; but Miss Charlotte said that she ought to have been named Discretion, like the fair damsel who belonged to the palace Beautiful, in the " Pilgrim's Progress."

It was an afternoon in May, and out of doors there was bright sunshine. But Henrietta and Charlotte Kemple were sitting in the cathedral-like gloom of their drawing-room, and did not see much of the sun. The front of the house was thickly covered with creepers, which hung in dense masses over the porch, and darkened all the windows. Sometimes a wandering wind would open a gap in the feathery foliage, and then a swift sunbeam would slip into the room, as if to reveal the fact that Henrietta was dozing over her knitting, and Charlotte reading a novel. They never indulged in dozing and fiction till the serious duties of the morning had all been conscientiously performed, and even then, Henrietta thought it necessary to apologize for her nap, and Charlotte for her story.

"It rests my eyes," said the elder sister, with a soft little sigh for her infirmities.

"It rests my mind," said the younger. "I am always trying to solve problems, you know, and the tale takes my attention off unanswerable questions."

So the afternoon stole gently away, and there was no one to watch—

"The flitting hand of the time-piece there,
In its close white bower of china flowers."

nor to see how the little Dresden china shepherd, in a court suit, prospered in his wooing of the shepherdess in her flowered robe and gilt shoes. They had spent years in mute courtship on the mantelpiece, and Joy, when she had carefully dusted them that very day, had wondered how old they were, and how much longer they would stand and smile insipidly at each other? For Joy's duties were so light nowadays, and she had so much time on her hands, that she was sometimes given to dreaming.

If you had seen her pacing the garden-walks in the afternoon sun, you would have said that she had very easily got over all her troubles. She was just the kind of young woman that one would associate with daisies and buttercups, and fresh green grass; and even after years of London life, a girl of her stamp will often retain a look of the country. Joy had grown thinner when she was worried and overworked at Notting Hill; but she was getting plump and comely again in this peaceful home at Richmond.

When Morris Durleigh had found her clinging to the railings in Savoy Street, he had firmly believed that she was on the verge of an illness. But a little comfort and kindness had restored her more quickly than had seemed possible. Quieting words, good food, and sound sleep had brought the colour back to her cheeks, and the light to her eyes, and she had begun to beg for work with all her heart. And then the Kemples were in want of a servant, and she seemed to have been created just for the purpose of living with two quiet old ladies. That was what Miss Charlotte said after only a short acquaintance with her new maid, and Miss Charlotte's judgment might generally be relied upon.

But did Joy herself feel that every want was satisfied in this safely-sheltered retreat? And had she indeed "got over" the loss of her life's faith and love?

The old garden was protected by high walls and higher trees. Sycamores caught the sunbeams on the tender green of their young leaves, and a great elm reared its branches against a sky of purest blue. All kinds of sweet old-fashioned flowers were blooming here; Joy welcomed the favourites of her childhood—anemones and gilliflowers, ranunculuses of burning gold, orange lilies lifting flame-coloured heads against a dark back-ground of ivied wall, large pansies, whose purple velvet might have made the robe of a fairy queen; and nearly at the end of the middle walk was a thick bed of lilies of the valley, an inexhaustible store of fragrant bells hidden away under their cool broad leaves.

Joy paused before the lily bed, and bent her head in silent thought, while the sun shone on the thick twists of yellow hair that were pinned up smoothly under her little cap. And then she moved on a few paces, for the garden ended in a great bower of lilacs and laburnums— mauve blossoms and golden pendants gently tossing and swaying together when the soft wind stirred them.

The girl lifted her hand, pulled down a heavy plume of lilac, and buried her face in the scented mass of bloom. She shut her eyes, and fancied that she was standing in the little garden that belonged to her grandfather's cottage. There was the well, and the great iron-bound bucket full of pure water, and the lilac-bush rising as high as the old thatch. And while she broke off boughs of lilac, a slim boy, with dark eyes, stood looking on, and laughing when she failed to reach the higher branches. Oh, George! If she could only hear him speak and laugh again!

Surely there is no time like "the merry May-time" for showing us visions of our vanished joys, and reviving our sense of loss with the breath of young blossoms. Many writers have told us (in many different phrases) that memories, old sentiments and associations, are more readily reached by the sense of smell than by any other channel. And of all the perfumes that set us dreaming of the past there is none more suggestive than the scent of lilac—that beautiful common shrub that grows just as well in the poor man's garden as in the rich man's grounds —a healthy plant, lavish of odour and blossom, asking little of its cultivator, and giving rich payment for small care. It was no wonder that this country girl, with sensitive heart and brain, should yield to the influence of its strong fragrance, and burst suddenly into a passion of tears.

Miss Charlotte, if she had been near, would have told her that it was very wrong to cry, that she ought to feel thankful for her deliverance from many snares and dangers, that her lover was a worthless, dishonest young man who did not deserve a single tear. All very true, perhaps; but is it not for the worthless things in our lives that the most plentiful tears are shed?

CHAPTER VI.

" I WILL TELL YOU WHEN THEY MET."

Joy was wise enough to check her tears before they got beyond her control. She gently released the lilac bough, and it started back into its place among the other branches, its blossoms still wet with her weeping. She could only do again what she had done a thousand times before—begin at the very beginning of the day when the purse was lost, and go thoughtfully over all the details of that miserable time. And there was nothing new to be extracted from her memory; nothing new that could shake her now firmly - rooted conviction of George's guilt.

She had been compelled to admit to herself that George had disappointed some of her expectations before the last blow fell. Down in the old village people had said that George Hunter might do well if he wasn't a rolling stone; and it had not seemed to her that town life had made him less unsettled. He was always fond of her, it is true; but had he ever loved her well enough to plod on steadily for her sake? A young man who really wants to marry will keep to the straightest road that leads to his heart's desire, let the way be ever so tame and dull. But George was constantly running off into by-ways, and finding that they led to no-where. Once or twice he had remarked that Joy had no high ambition. A trim little cottage with a garden, the housework to do, George to love, a child to nurse and toil for, would have realized all her brightest dreams of future happiness. But George, although this tranquil prospect had looked fair in his eyes, was not without aspirations.

Sometimes she had thought that she was too simple and countrified to satisfy him; but then an affectionate word or loving look would set her heart at rest. And sometimes she had fancied that he was growing reserved and mysterious, and no longer cared to make a *confidante* of his little rustic sweetheart; but she had never seen him so strange— so unnatural and constrained—as he had been on the day of their last meeting.

Morris Durleigh and his daughter had listened patiently to her story from its very commencement. They had heard the evidence against George many times,

and both had tried—Godiva especially—
not to believe him guilty. But it had
struck them both that poor Joy had
really known very little about her lover's
life after he had left Cathrington; and
by his own confession it had been proved
to have been a most unsettled life. They
said as gently as possible what they
thought. George had yielded to a sudden
temptation when the bag was put into
his hands. He had been, very likely, in
great need of money, and he had allowed
an evil impulse to conquer him. Afterwards—well, afterwards he had had to
accept the consequences of his crime,
and disappear without leaving a trace
behind him.

"I can't change anything," thought
Joy, wiping her eyes carefully. "I hope
Miss Charlotte won't find out that I've
been crying. It really does seem un-

grateful to cry in such a pleasant place as this. I never could have expected as much peace and comfort as I have found here."

She went back along the flower-bordered paths to the house, and entered just as the clock was striking four. At that moment there came a ring which roused the old ladies out of their drowsy calm, and Joy opened the hall-door. Godiva Durleigh, fresh and smiling, was waiting outside with her father.

"Oh, Joy, how well you are looking!" she said.

Morris Durleigh gave the girl a keen glance and a kind smile; and then the visitors were ushered into the dim drawing-room. They found Henrietta waking up softly in her easy-chair, and Charlotte, bright-eyed and alert, standing bolt upright to receive them.

Morris had a great deal to say to the sisters about a Home for destitute children, and two little ones who had been lately placed in it at their expense. Godiva knew all that could be told about the Home, and she was possessed with a girl's longing for flowers and sunshine. Charlotte, always quick, divined her feeling in a moment.

"Go out into the garden, my dear," she said, "and get a good handful of lilies. We will call you when tea is ready."

That old garden always seemed to Godiva Durleigh to be an earthly paradise, where sweet things had been growing, and slowly coming to perfection years before she was born. Who were the men and women who had walked here long ago? The girl went dreaming on about them, looking at the delicate leaf-

sprays and light shadows trembling all
around her.

> " Here there was laughing of old, there was
> weeping
> Haply of lovers none ever will know."

What vows had been whispered under
the lilac boughs, she wondered ? If one
could only learn flower-and-leaf language
and understand the stories that the trees
and blossoms told each other ! Godiva
had inherited her father's warm heart
and sensitive nature ; but she was gifted
with more imagination than he had ever
possessed. Some day she meant to write
a tale about the Kemples' old garden ;
already she had pencilled a few verses in
praise of this favourite haunt of hers ;
but they were locked up securely in her
desk, and no one had ever seen them.

She had nearly reached the end of
the middle path when she heard foot-

steps, and turned to see who was coming.

It was not, as she had half tried to believe, a gentleman of the old school in a prune-coloured coat and lace cravat and ruffles, but only a tall young man in modern attire. He had a pleasant face with good features, and a clear olive complexion, and carried himself with a certain graceful ease. Altogether he was not unfit to be the hero of a girl's romance, as far as appearance went; and little Godiva thought that he looked darkly handsome and interesting. She had never seen him before, but the Kemples had made her well acquainted with his photograph. The old ladies had so few relations left that they took a great pride in their only nephew, and hung portraits of him in every room in their house.

He came up to Godiva, lifted his hat, and addressed her with a grave courtesy which sat very well on him.

"May I introduce myself, Miss Durleigh? I am Rex Longworthy. My aunt Charlotte has sent me here to find you."

"I have heard them speak of you very often," said the girl frankly.

"Ah, they have not many people to talk about!" A kindly gleam lit up the grave dark face. "I have never met you here before, but I generally come to see my aunts on Sundays. I think it must be Sunday here all the week long. What a peaceful old place this is!"

"It is charming," said Godiva. "Not a bit like the ordinary suburban garden, where everything is so painfully neat and new; and the rose-trees are labelled, and the variegated foliage is harshly brilliant!

All that one finds here has had plenty
of time to grow, instead of being hurried
and worried into bloom and leafage."

"I wonder how long it will stay as it
is?" remarked the young man thoughtfully. "I should like to think that it
will be the same ten years hence. But
that's too much to expect, isn't it?"

"Perhaps it will be watched over by
some guardian angel," she suggested.

"Who will be strong enough to resist
the destroying 'angel of the age. Well,
we will hope so; but I have seen so
many bowery old scenes changed to
bricks and mortar that I can't be sanguine."

He did not look as if he could be
sanguine about anything, she thought,
as she quietly studied his face. He had
no beard, and his moustache did not
entirely conceal the grave, patient ex-

pression of the firm lips. The Kemples had said that he was only two and twenty, but he looked older, sadder, and stronger than a man generally looks at that age. It was a face that suggested power and self-restraint, and seemed to indicate that these forces had been early called into play. Godiva had inherited her father's gift as a physiognomist, and learnt later that all which she had read in Rex's countenance was verily written there.

As to Rex, he was thinking what a bright sympathetic little girl she was; and how he liked the transparent grey eyes that looked calmly and straightforwardly at everything from under their black lashes. They were as clear as a child's eyes, yet they were not childish. In thinking over that evening long afterwards he felt that there was a springtide freshness, not only in the garden, but in the girl who walked with a quiet joy among the flowers. Godiva was able to enjoy things thoroughly, and draw all their sweetness out of them because she could forget herself. If she was effective, it was not the result of studying effects; and yet there were men, well trained in society's ways, who would have said that the result somehow *had* been attained without study.

It was a proof of her sympathetic nature that Rex began to talk to her about the old places he had loved, and seldom spoke of. She had the rare power of stimulating people, and making them give out the best of themselves. She listened with such a bright, clear look, and uttered now and then such a soft little exclamation of interest, that he was drawn on to speak of his past life freely; so freely, that he wondered afterwards at himself.

"This is the sweetest old garden that I have ever seen, save one," he said. "My grandfather's rectory garden was like this. There were thick bushes of rosemary and lavender there, just like those yonder; and his cedars were as fine as these. I dare say the ground was wanted badly enough for a new school-house; but I can never quite forgive them for the desolation they made."

"And your grandfather? How he must miss his garden!"

"I hope he doesn't; no, I don't think he does." Rex's voice had a ring in it that moved her. "He was dead before they began to carry out their plans; they would not touch the garden while he lived."

"And could they not really do without it?" Godiva asked.

"I believe not. The rectory stands in the midst of a great overcrowded town, a town that keeps on growing and growing till one wonders what it will come to at last. Every foot of ground is precious there, and it was hard for the poor children to be packed into their close schoolrooms, while my grandfather owned a wide paradise, carefully walled in. Yes, I suppose they were right when they decided that the little kids were worth more than grass and flowers and old trees."

"Quite right." Godiva's soft voice took a clear decided tone. "Something always has to be sacrificed when good is to be done. Doing the right thing is sure to be rather hard, I think."

"You don't know how hard."

The words seemed to come unawares.
Then he looked at her, and his mouth
and eyes relaxed into a smile.

"I know I have had little experience,"
she said meekly. "When I think of the
things that people have given up because
it was not right to keep them, I wonder
at their courage."

"Well, I hope it will never be proved
that it is wrong to keep this old garden."
He spoke in a lighter tone. "It belongs
to my aunts, you know, and they love it
dearly. If ever I had to go away from
England I should like to know it would
be here, just the same, when I came
back. I suppose I feel that it is the
last of the old flowery places left to me."

So they lingered in the sun and shade,
and talked on, growing better acquainted
every minute, until Miss Charlotte came
briskly down the long middle path to

summon them to tea. Most old maids
are either match-makers or match-spoil-
ers; and Miss Charlotte belonged unconsciously to the first class, although she
had never had many opportunities of
bringing her powers into play.

When she looked down the green vista,
and saw the two figures advancing, softly
flecked with lights and shadows, a sentimental feeling took possession of her
mind at once. How nice it would be
if this pair were to take a fancy to each
other, she thought. Supposing that this
garden-path, with its over-arching boughs
and delicate blossoms, should lead to
that long-life path where two may walk
happily and safely, clinging closely to
each other to the end!

If a woman has had no romance in
her own life, she is apt to look for it in
the lives of others. Charlotte was less

amiable than Henrietta, but her imagination was more vivid, and she had felt
the lack of romance more keenly than
her sister had ever done. It was not
the pretty dove-like Henrietta who had
wanted to be loved and married; it
was the plain, sharp-tongued Charlotte.
And, alas! the sharp tongue had driven
away friends that the warm heart would
have given the world to keep!—men,
who might have become lovers, had been
kept at arm's length by one who would
gladly have drawn them nearer, if she
had but known how to do it.

And so it had come to pass that the
young men of Charlotte's youth had gone
off to other maidens who could say soft
words and sigh. And Charlotte, brusque
as ever, trod her solitary way with such
a spirited air that no one ever believed
she did not enjoy being an old maid.

"She was meant to be a spinster," said the lookers-on who think they know everything. "As to Henrietta, it was clear that she was single by mistake. What a lovely, tender wife and mother Henrietta Kemple would have made, if she had married in her young days!" Thus spoke those who judge "by the outer appearance;" but it needed a diviner sight to see that the soft, self-indulgent nature could never have adapted itself happily to the exactions of a husband. It was Charlotte who could have given, freely and gladly, a wife's unselfish help and generous love.

"They shall have every opportunity that I can give them," she thought, glowing with secret pleasure. "But I shall not say one word to Henrietta. Dear Henrietta loves to do good and give money to the poor; but she isn't interested in the affairs of young people. She doesn't care for novels, which are nothing but love-affairs in volumes. It was always to me that Louisa turned for sympathy when Captain Longworthy was courting her. I dare say I oughtn't to have encouraged her as I did—Joseph and Henrietta both blamed me—but I have my weak points. It is a blessing that dear Rex is not much like his father!"

She went up to the young pair, her little brown eyes twinkling. Godiva was looking very well that day in a soft grey gown which fitted closely to her slender, pliant figure; her chestnut hair rippled under her straw hat. Never until that moment had Charlotte thought her pretty; but to-day, in her fresh youth and gladness, she seemed suddenly to have bloomed into beauty.

"Have you forgotten the lilies?" asked Miss Charlotte, archly. "I see you have not gathered any yet. Never mind, you can get some by-and-by. It seems a shame to leave the garden yet and come indoors, doesn't it? But it is not warm enough to bring the tea-table out here, and Henrietta easily catches cold."

"I don't think you ever catch cold, aunty," said Rex, laying his hand caressingly on her shoulder.

"Not often," she admitted. "I am ever so much stronger than Henrietta. Beautiful people are generally delicate, I fancy. Your mother was delicate, Rex; and she was lovely, you know."

"I know; I can remember her," he said gravely. "She was not much like Aunt Henrietta; mother's eyes were a darker blue."

"Not as dark as yours," remarked Aunt Charlotte, glancing up at her tall nephew with a loving look.

Godiva involuntarily looked at him, too, and made a discovery. His eyes were neither black nor brown, but violet; rich with all possible depths, and prone to sudden lights that gleamed out unexpectedly from under dark lashes. She looked away again but remembered them.

They went into the house, and found the old silver teapot and the red-and-blue cups and saucers awaiting them in the dim drawing-room. Rex handed cups, and Godiva sat on an ottoman close to Miss Henrietta's easy-chair. Morris Durleigh, a little tired with earnest talking, was leaning back in a corner of the sofa, and looking quietly at them all, without seeing them.

In this house there was always a pleasant silence; you could hear the birds chirping in the creepers all the time people were speaking. The window stood open as far as the old-fashioned sash would go; slender sprays and tendrils swayed in a soft breeze; the sunshine flickered on the walls of the old room, with its faded needlework and prim furniture. Long years afterwards the sweet atmosphere of that room used to come round about Rex and Godiva when they were miles away from Richmond. The heart may forget its storms, but always retains the memory of its times of peace.

The young people strayed out-of-doors again, and returned with a prodigious bunch of flowers. Miss Charlotte met them with a triumphant smile, and told Godiva that she had been settling something.

"Your father has given his consent," she said. "You are to come to us next Sunday, and stay till Monday. We have arranged it all."

"But he cannot spare me; I never leave him!" cried the girl, with a wistful look at the worn face she loved so well.

"Oh yes, he can spare you for a little while," Miss Charlotte insisted. "You are pale; young girls should always have a holiday in May."

"And we shall meet again," said Rex, with grave satisfaction. "I am sure to be here on Sunday."

CHAPTER VII.

REX'S EARLY DAYS.

HENRIETTA and Charlotte Kemple had an only brother, who preferred his gloomy chambers in the City to the flowery little house at Richmond. Joseph was the eldest of the family, and had acted, after the father's death, as guardian to his three sisters. He had never married, and having formed a bad opinion of husbands in general, had never desired the girls to marry. Henrietta, a woman after his own heart, had always opposed a gentle indifference to the advances of all her admirers; Charlotte had frightened hers away; but Louisa, the youngest and prettiest, allowed herself to be easily wooed, and far too quickly won.

Of all her suitors (and she had many) Captain Longworthy was the last whom her friends would have had her choose. He was a Charles Surface, handsome, gay, rollicking, and extravagant; a soldier of a common type, with all the faults and some of the virtues of his class. The Kemples might perhaps have more readily forgiven the faults and esteemed the virtues, if Louisa's lover had not committed the one unpardonable sin of looking down upon them. But Horace Longworthy had inherited the military contempt for tradespeople, and, passionately as he loved Louisa, he could never quite succeed in forgetting that she was a City merchant's daughter.

In spite of Joseph's warnings and

Henrietta's gentle expostulations, the courtship went on. Charlotte was first on one side and then on the other, and so earned the reproaches of both parties. But the romance of the affair was too much for her at last, and she ended in taking Louisa's part and fighting her battle with all the energy of her character.

So Louisa was married to her hero, and was received, with stately courtesy, by his father, the rector, and his grandfather, the general. She was refined — interesting — beautiful — and won the hearts of all the Longworthys before her husband took her away to India.

The Kemples were very sad after her departure. She had said to her people, " Give me my portion," and had taken it, and was gone away out of their lives for ever. In a few years the portion was gone, too. Horace Longworthy loved his wife, but he squandered her money. One or two babies were born and died, and then Louisa's married life came suddenly to an end. There was an unexpected outbreak of the fierce hill-tribes; a quick call to arms; a brilliant charge, and Horace fell at the head of his men, gay, dashing, gallant to the last.

The rest may be briefly told. Little Rex, the only surviving child, came home with his mother to the rectory, where the grey-headed rector mourned his son alone. The Kemples travelled to the noisy Midland town to see their sister, and found her looking like the ghost of the beautiful, sunshiny girl who had left them. She met them with affection, but clung with pathetic tenderness to the father of her dead husband. Rex was naughty, and refused to be friendly with the strange aunts. They went back to the little house at Richmond with many tears, feeling that although Louisa had come again to England, she was as far away from them in spirit as ever.

And yet her heart was not so utterly sundered from them as they believed. If she had lived long enough to overcome her sorrow, and win back her strength, she would have been the sister of old days once more. But grief and the Indian climate had utterly wrecked her health, and even in the peaceful atmosphere of the rectory she did not rally. The sight of her boy, growing strong and beautiful, with his father's dark complexion, and her own violet eyes, only deepened the anguish of regret.

Once again the quiet women at Richmond travelled to the Midland town, and took their last farewell of Louisa. And

then they knew that she loved them still
—had always loved them, even when she
had seemed to forget. Little Rex, she
said, must stay with his grandfather while
the old man lived; this had been her
husband's wish. But Henrietta and
Charlotte would not forget that he was
their own little nephew, would they?
Indeed, they would know that she had
taught him to love them all—his Uncle
Joseph too.

Afterwards it was in his aunt Charlotte's
arms that little Rex wept away the first
anguish of his loss. It wrung the hearts
of these good women to go back to
Richmond leaving the boy behind. But
when the first outburst of grief was over,
Rex showed no desire to forsake the
rectory. His mother, dear as she was,
had always been a feeble invalid, not
strong enough to play with him; and the

old rector had made the child his com-
panion.

There was something touching in the
little fellow's affection for his grandfather; and although the rectory was a
sombre home for a child, it was never
unhappy. There were no noisy games
nor juvenile parties, but the boy always
felt that he was loved, and that quiet
consciousness seemed to satisfy him.
The rector had never taken much trouble
about all the souls committed to his care
in the great straggling parish. He did
not belong to the " earnest " school; but
was a clergyman of the old type—
courtly, scholarly, and indolent,—and if
the " hungry sheep looked up and were
not fed," so much the worse for them.
He had only the driest kind of spiritual
food to give them. No one had ever
believed him to be a man of strong

affections, and yet it was certain that he lavished a wealth of quiet tenderness upon the child.

After his grandfather, little Rex would be the last of the Longworthys. The general had died, leaving no children; Horace was gone; and there was only the little Indian-born lad to bear the old name and wear it honourably. It was a name that had been well-known in military annals; Longworthy after Longworthy had won a soldier's laurels and found a soldier's grave; and the strongest desire of Rex's heart was to be a soldier.

It was a proof of the rector's indolence that he took no steps to gratify the boy's wish. Death came to him suddenly and painlessly when Rex was sixteen, and it was very soon known that the old man had little to leave his grandson.

Mr. Longworthy, quietly as he had

lived, had never denied himself anything. The best wines, and all the choicest delicacies of the seasons, were always to be found on his table ; and he had been in the habit of entertaining his old college friends. No man knew better how to give a dinner ; but the pity was, that the dinners were never given to those who were in need of a meal. It was a pleasure to see the stately, white-haired old clergyman sitting at the head of his board ; a pleasure to hear the clever old-world stories that he told so well ; a pleasure to watch the graceful ease and tact which made his guests so happy in his presence, and so thoroughly in harmony with each other. So pleasant was all this, that one was in danger of forgetting the poverty and misery that pressed close up to the rectory walls. And Rex, sitting modestly among his elders, and silently enjoying himself, did, indeed, forget all the want and shame and sin that lay just outside his grandfather's door.

When all was over, and the boy was alone in the old house, after the funeral, his uncle, Joseph Kemple, came to see him.

Rex had always cherished his childhood's love for his mother's sisters, and had written to them regularly and often. But he had never seen his uncle Joseph until now, and his first impression of this unknown relative was not favourable.

First, he found himself wondering how such pretty women as his Aunt Henrietta and his mother came to have such a plain brother. Secondly, he felt a sudden conviction that Joseph Kemple was a complete impersonation of all the disagreeable qualities which have dis-

tinguished the bad uncles of fiction, from
the heartless kinsman of the Babes in
the Wood downwards. Thirdly, he resolved that he would endure any rough
treatment from other hands, rather than
submit for an hour to the rule of this
obnoxious man.

But none of these feelings were betrayed in the lad's manner and face. He
stood up, straight and tall, and dressed
in deep mourning, looking very much
like a young hero of romance. He seemed
to have modelled himself upon his grandfather, and received Uncle Joseph with
that self-possessed and stately courtesy
which had always marked the rector.

It would be untrue to say that Joseph
was quite unmoved by the grand air of
his nephew. He was a little amused,
and a little disconcerted. It would, he
felt, be no easy matter to deal with this

grave and courteous boy, who looked at him with such honest seriousness, and gave him a chair with such graceful formality. If the rector had left nothing else to his grandson, he had bequeathed his good manner to the lad, and it was a possession that was likely to last a lifetime.

To eyes that had seen a good deal of the world, Joseph Kemple would have seemed an every-day City man, more old-fashioned than his fellows, but quite able to march with the times. He was not pompous, he never patronized even a pauper; but he had his own peculiar set of opinions, and stuck to them firmly. As to "manner," he had been so unmindful of William of Wykham's maxim, that he had never thought about it at all. He had come to say something to his nephew, and the sooner it was said and done with the better.

"Rex," he began abruptly, "I had a long talk with your aunts before I came here, and they thoroughly agree with all that I shall say to you. It won't sound pleasant, I suppose; common sense seldom does. But I mean to insure your good if I can."

The young fellow bowed slightly, but did not speak.

"You know that the rector had nothing to leave but his plate and furniture, and books?" the other went on. "All this has already been made quite clear to you, has it not?"

"Quite clear," was the quiet reply.

"I know that you have set your heart upon entering the service," said Joseph, clearing his throat. "You have said so many times in your letters to Richmond, and your aunts always regretted this inclination. But you now know that you cannot carry out your plan without getting friends to help you with money?"

A dark flush mounted to the lad's forehead. His heart was beginning to throb at a wild pace, but he managed to preserve an outward calm.

"Mr. Mansell has said something of the kind," he answered after a slight pause.

"Mansell is a good lawyer; I had a chat with him in his office this morning," said Joseph. "His brother, in London, is an old acquaintance of mine. And I want you to understand that the proposal I am about to make is warmly approved by Mansell."

Again Rex bowed in silence.

"I am willing to take you into my business," continued his uncle, speaking impressively, "and to give you just such a position as you would have had if you.

had been my son. If you do well I shall leave you all that I have—and that will be something considerable. Does this prospect please you?"

"You are too good, sir," said the boy, and his voice shook a little. "Don't think that I do not appreciate your kindness. But—no, I'm not fit for business."

"Any lad with decent brains can make himself fit for business," Joseph replied.

"Most can; but I cannot," Rex answered gravely. "My heart follows my father's calling. I must be a soldier; I have never dreamt of being anything else."

"And out of your magnificent pay you will have to pay back borrowed money," said Joseph, coldly. "Do you realize that you will be always cramped in means—always practising wretched little economies, or getting into debt? Surely you must see that a man should never enter the service unless he has a fair income of his own?"

"I must go on as well as I can," returned Rex, drawing a long breath. "It will be hard, I daresay; but not so hard as a life that has no charm."

"Do you suppose the charm will last?" inquired Joseph, with a slight sneer.

"Yes, sir, I do." The boy's violet eyes shone. "My father never regretted that he was a soldier. The men of my family have fought in all the great battles; we are a military race, and we can't make good civilians. Put us in front of the enemy at the head of our men, and we don't do badly!"

Something rose up in Joseph's throat, and checked him as he was going to speak. Rex had looked so like his mother at that moment that the shrewd man of business passed over the boyish enthusiasm, and thought only of the sister who had been so well loved. Just so had Louisa looked and spoken when she had declared her intention of marrying Horace Long-worthy. But he did not want to be softened just then, and Rex, in his enthusiastic mood, could never be brought to hear reason. The interview must be ended, and the subject dropped for the present.

"Well, Rex," he said, rising, "I will leave you to think over my offer, and if you change your mind you can let me know. Only understand that I shall do nothing for you if you persist in having your whim."

The lad coloured angrily at the word "whim;" but his self-control did not desert him. He thanked his uncle again, sent a loving message to his aunts at

Richmond, and took leave of Joseph with a sad dignity that his youth made pathetic. Joseph went away, admiring his nephew against his will, and turned his steps to Mansell's office.

The lawyer was putting on his hat to go home, and met him with a smile.

" You haven't succeeded with the lad, I suppose ? ' he said.

" No," admitted Kemple gravely.

" Well, don't give him up just yet. Let me have a word or two with his highness before you despair of him," Mansell pleaded. " Perhaps I may bring him to a right mind."

CHAPTER VIII.

"GOD HATH ALREADY SAID WHAT SHALL BETIDE."

The lawyer resolved to set about the business of bringing Rex to reason that very evening. He dined at six, thinking about the boy as he drank his claret, and answering all Mrs. Mansell's questions in monosyllables. He had no son; his daughter was married, and lived miles away; there were no family cares to absorb his thoughts; and, in spite of the hardening influence of years of professional life, he really did take a genuine human interest in Rex Longworthy.

On this June evening the whole population of the noisy town seemed to have made up its mind to come out of doors. It was a grimy population, given to slouching outside public-houses, and leaning heavily against door-posts when its day's work was done. The walls of the rectory garden, high and strong enough to had protected a convent, were decorated with cartoons in white chalk, the performances of juvenile artists, who swarmed about the place — poor pallid children who had never, even on feast-days, caught a glimpse of the paradise within those walls. Mansell heard the people talking to each other as he passed along. Already there were rumours of approaching changes. They were saying that the walls would soon come down ; now that the old rector was gone the new schools would be built upon the garden ground. Nobody spoke regretfully of the old man ; the solitary mourner in the silent house had none to share his grief.

The lawyer was shown into the study, a room in which the late Mr. Longworthy had spent a great deal of his time. It was a remarkably pleasant room, old-fashioned and sombre, but always warm in the evening with the last sunshine of the day. The windows reaching to the ground, opened into a verandah supported by slender pillars. Every column was wreathed with roses, climbing up eagerly to the roof, and there mingling with a mass of foliage. The study was full of perfumes, and the rector's old china bowls were freshly filled with the flowers that he had liked best in his lifetime. Everything in the study looked so precisely the same as it always had done, that Mansell was almost startled by the absence of change.

Rex was sitting under the verandah in his grandfather's cane chair, leaning back on the cushions in an easy attitude of indolence. His hands were folded on his knees—the hands of an idle boy, beautifully-shaped, smooth, olive-skinned ; his eyes were gazing dreamily into the green alleys, touched with sunset gold.

" Dear me, this is a very puzzling lad," thought the lawyer. " Anglo-Indian in his lounging ways. He sits there as if he were going to stay always in the place, and looks as much at his ease as if he had just come into a fortune. The talk with his uncle doesn't seem to have disturbed him in the least."

But when Rex rose slowly from the depths of the easy-chair, and stood up to receive him, Mansell was not so sure about his perfect serenity. There were shadows under his eyes, that made them

darker than before, and the lips were
firmly compressed, as if he were forcing
himself to endure pain without a murmur.

" I thought I should find you alone this
evening, my boy," said Mansell, with the
familiarity of an old friend. " Don't leave
your seat. It's delightful out here among
the roses, and one can see the sunset.
So you had a visit from Mr. Kemple
to-day ? "

" Yes," replied Rex, gravely.

" And you declined his offer ? You are
still bent on being a soldier ? "

" Yes."

" Ah ! " Mansell leaned back in his
seat and looked musingly across the
flower-beds. " Of course it would be
hard for you to give up your heart's
desire ; it's quite natural that you should
cling to it. But you will need money,
you see ? "

"I have been thinking of that," said Rex, in a quiet voice. "I wish I could manage without a loan," he added, knitting his smooth brows; "but I'm afraid it's impossible."

"Quite impossible, as I have already explained. Have you thought of any one to apply to?"

The lad flushed, and paused a moment before he asked the question.

"I have decided to ask Major Wallington," he said at last. "I don't like it, mind. You understand that I don't like it, Mr. Mansell."

The lawyer inclined his head, and looked at him keenly.

"Isn't there any one else, Rex?" he asked.

"There's no one else. Major Wallington is quite a rich man, you know; and very few of my grandfather's friends were

rich. Then, too, I am the Major's god-
son. My father wrote to him from India,
asking him to be godfather; and he consented, and has always taken a great
interest in me. I believe he will be ready
to help me."

" I believe he will," responded Mansell,
gravely. " He will help you, even if he
suffers for it. But it is possible that you
have not heard of his altered circumstances ? "

" Circumstances ? " Rex was startled.
He propped his chin on his hand and
gazed anxiously at the lawyer with
gloomy eyes. " What has happened ? " he
asked.

" On the day before the rector died
a great Indian bank broke," replied Mansell, in a calm, impressive tone. " Major
Wallington was implicated in the failure,
and when everything is settled he will

find his income much reduced. I am really sorry. He has only one child— a pretty girl, who is engaged to be married."

"Yes; I know Ida. Are you quite sure that the news is true?"

"Quite sure, Rex. I wish there was a doubt. But there is none."

The boy was pale now; but he was as undemonstrative as ever. Leaning back in his chair, he thoughtfully caressed his upper lip in silence. The lawyer watched him narrowly with half-closed eyes.

The pause was a long one. Slowly the golden lights were fading and changing, and the first soft shades of grey were filling up the nooks and corners of the old garden. A sleepy bird sent forth a smothered chirp now and then; occasionally a hoarse sound from the ever-restless

town reached their ears; but Mansell
had never realized the peace and stillness
of the rectory as he realized it now. It
was to keep this peace to the end of his
days that the rector had been deaf to
all complaints about the overcrowded
schools. He would not voluntarily yield
an inch of his guarded paradise. The
lawyer looked furtively at Rex, who was
sitting erect and quiet, with a face as
darkly still as if it had belonged to a
bronze statue instead of a boy. He
wondered whether the lad had inherited
his grandfather's calm selfishness?

"Major Wallington isn't quite a
pauper, Rex," he said. "I don't want to
misrepresent the matter. I only thought
it right to let you know that he is likely
to be cramped just now. Still, he would
make an effort for you; there can be no
doubt of that."

Rex turned his head slowly, and there was a light on his sombre face.

"Yes, he would make an effort," he repeated quietly. "But I'm not going to let him do that."

There was no mistaking the ring of determination in the young voice. Mansell's keenest interest was aroused; he was quite eager to know what was coming next.

"Is there any one else in your mind?" he asked. "If so you had better tell me. I know more about men's affairs than you do, of course; and I can say in a moment whether there is any hope from this quarter or that."

"There's no one else." Rex spoke with frank simplicity. "If my godfather can't help me, I shan't apply to another man."

"Ah," said Mansell, a little vaguely,

"I see. That is, I *don't* exactly see what course you mean to take."

"Nor do I," the boy returned with a half-smile. "Not this evening. To-morrow there may be light on my way."

His face grew grave again while he was speaking. His own words, uttered without thought, had wakened an un-expected echo in his own heart. "Lead, kindly light," the echo seemed to say; and the hymn which has, since it was first written, expressed the passionate pleadings of thousands of souls, became for the first time the prayer of this proud young spirit. He did not even know at that moment that it was really a prayer. He thought it was merely a remembrance of some favourite lines (Rex had always appreciated good poetry); only the words had come to him with a new strength, and with a feeling that was a blending of sweetness and stinging pain.

He was alone, and the "encircling gloom" was deepening on every side. He had chosen his own path, never doubting that it was the right path for him to tread, marked as it was by the footprints of his race, and illumined by that stormy splendour which always dazzles young eyes. And now he saw plainly enough that it was not the way for him to walk in.

"Well, good-bye," said Mansell, rising. "If any idea does happen to occur to you, let me know to-morrow morning. There's nothing like thinking a matter well over. It wouldn't do any harm, I fancy, just to give Mr. Kemple's proposal another thought or two; but after all you must judge for yourself, and I see you've a cool head on your young shoulders."

He went his way; and, instead of going straight home, called at the hotel where Joseph Kemple was staying.

"There isn't much of old Longworthy in that young fellow," he said. "It's worth while to have a little patience with him. I think you'll get him into your way yet. And if once he puts his hand to your plough there will be no looking back. If he makes his choice he'll stick to it."

"Well, I hope he will," Joseph answered. "My sisters would do anything to keep him near them. As for myself, I wasn't particularly anxious to have a boy to look after. But as he belongs to me, I naturally wish to do my best for him. And he shan't be a swaggering spendthrift, puffed up with infernal pride, as his father was! Not if I can help it."

Mansell smiled.

"Horace Longworthy was a fine fellow in his way," he remarked.

"Much too fine for me," said Kemple, grimly. "But Rex is Lousia's child," he added, softening. "He is a good deal like her sometimes. And his aunts have made up their minds that he's to be the pride of the family. I shouldn't like them to be disappointed."

"I don't think they will be disappointed," replied the lawyer in a tone of quiet conviction.

Meanwhile the lad whom they were discussing sat alone in the summer twilight, and silently fought the first battle of his life.

He knew more of his father's history than any one supposed. A great many details had been gathered from an old servant who had been with them in India, and had nursed his mother through her last illness. He had learnt that there had been ceaseless troubles arising out of money-matters;—that if his wife had come to him empty-handed, Horace Longworthy could not have got on at all;—that, as it was, the husband had spent everything. Rex had pondered over all these things; and he was old enough now to see that there were spots on the sun of his father's glory.

One fact was quite clear in his mind: it was a bad thing to carry a sword if you had nothing beyond your pay to depend upon. Still worse would it be if you entered the service hampered with a loan, which you must repay out of your slender means. But surely the worst thing of all would be to give up your heart's desire,—sacrifice the career you had pictured for yourself—and go quietly into trade.

He started up, turned into the study, and stood on the hearth-rug. Then, all alone in the dusk, he drew himself up to his full height, and held his head all the more loftily because he must bend it by-and-by. It was too dark to distinguish the faces of the portraits on the walls; but he knew them all by heart, and was exceedingly well acquainted with that bright youth in uniform who hung over the mantelpiece. That was a certain Herbert Longworthy, who had fought under Wellington at Waterloo, and had been mortally wounded there. But he had lived long enough to hear that his great chief made honourable mention of him; and then had fallen asleep "like a warrior taking his rest." Rex had never envied the lad as he did at this moment. For *him* there was no miserable struggle; —no bitter doubt and anxiety. He had been bred a soldier; he had done his part; and gone triumphantly to his laurel-crowned grave.

But in that young hero's days the Longworthys had been a wealthier family. And now the last of the race, feeling very helpless and lonely, was standing in this empty room, and fighting a stern fight with no audible voice to cheer him on. For a little while he felt passionately angry with Joseph Kemple. If his uncle had really wanted to befriend him, why had he not given him money enough to carry out his long-cherished purpose? But, on second thoughts, was not that expecting a little too much of Joseph, who had been civilly sneered at and trampled upon by his military brother-in-law? And had not Louisa Longworthy, in her last days, let fall many words of loving regret about the brother and sisters, whose affection, although slighted, had never failed? Yes; Rex could not help feeling a tenderness towards these despised Kemples, who wanted to be good to him, and provide for him in their own way.

He was very lonely; yet gradually, and after a long struggle, there came to him a sense of being helped to a decision.

When at last the conflict was over he found himself almost in darkness in the room. Out in the garden the leaves were whispering in the starlight, and he heard a sound of closing doors and drawing bolts which told him that the old butler was shutting up the house for the night.

The mental strife had left him tired in body and mind. He felt that the time had come for breaking all the links that still held him to the past. And he resolved, then and there, that he would not linger in the old rectory any longer than was necessary. The new life must be begun at once, if it was to be begun at all.

CHAPTER IX.

DREAMS AND SUNSHINE.

IT was one of those May mornings when the young summer finds her way into the nooks and corners of the city, and fills every bit of space with verdure and sunlight and song. Even to Barnard's Inn this glory had come, and the plane-trees in the quadrangle were arrayed in their newest green. Every leaf was delicately fresh ; sparrows were twittering merrily on the boughs, and in the trimly kept garden there were geraniums lighting up the dusky spot with their vivid colours.

When the hero of " Great Expectations " affirmed that the melancholy little
square of Barnard's Inn looked to him
like " a flat burying-ground " he was
hardly just to the place. At first, while
city life was still new, Rex had spent
some gloomy hours in his sitting-room
overlooking the quadrangle. When the
trees were stripped of leaves, and gusts
of wind whirled straws and dust and
scraps of rubbish in dreary dances along
the silent side-walk, he had felt a bitter
craving for the rectory garden of old
times. And he had wondered why he
had tamely consented to live in the
rooms which his uncle had found for
him? Could not Joseph Kemple have
selected some brighter spot than this
secluded nook where everything seemed
quietly going to decay?

But perhaps the consciousness that he

was not compelled to live here made the place .endurable. Uncle Joseph was by no means a tyrant. If his nephew had found fault with these quarters, there were others to be had. Yet Rex stayed on without complaint, and gradually discovered that he was growing attached to Barnard's Inn, and did not want to leave it.

The sitting-room had two windows, with many panes, and each was furnished with its box of flowers, so that stray visitors, looking up from outside, beheld two little gardens in the air. It was not a large room, but it held Rex's belongings comfortably. His piano stood in one corner; his books were everywhere; his photographs hung on the walls in simple oak frames. The mantelpiece was draped in an artistic fashion, and a luxurious chair on each side of the fireplace told that Rex still clung to his old love of ease. He had parted with the dream of his boyhood, but not with his earliest influences. His grandfather's graceful bearing and never-failing courtesy were reproduced in this young man who spent his days in a city office. His associates did not always understand him, and did not always like him; but they respected him.

Something in the freshness of the May morning, and the play of sunbeams and zephyrs among the leaves, had sent his thoughts back into the past. The tea was cooling on the breakfast-table while he stood dreaming at the open window —going off into a vague dream about dreams.

He remembered that when he first came here he had looked often across the quadrangle to the house that was opposite to his own. In that old house the last of the alchemists had lived and died; and Rex had sometimes wondered what changes would have been wrought in the world if Peter Woulfe's dreams had been realized. He had pictured the dim room encumbered with furnaces and strange apparatus, and the eager-faced man toiling day after day after the unattainable.

How long, and oh, how vainly, had Woulfe striven to discover the elixir of life! Rex could fancy the enthusiast's wild joy when he had believed himself to be on the verge of success, and the cold gloom of ever-recurring disappointment. In that quiet room, whose window was now hidden by the leafy boughs, the fruitless toil had ended; and perhaps (who can say?) the spirit, freed from the flesh, had found out that great secret

at last. Was it worth while to waste
a mortal life in trying to discover what
the immortal life would assuredly reveal ?
Why not have enjoyed the common joys
of earth, and waited calmly till the in-
effable wisdom was given ?

The birds broke out into a merrier
burst than ever, and a light seemed to
flash suddenly over the young fellow's
sombre face. Not many miles away there
was an earthly paradise of blossom and
song, and a young girl wandering among
the flowers. Rex whistled a tuneful
answer to the sparrows, and turned to
his neglected breakfast with gladness of
heart.

"People may say that Morris Durleigh
is as wild a dreamer as poor old Woulfe
was," he thought. "And they may say,
too—with some truth—that he takes
little thought about the future of his

daughter. But it is good to see how the girl believes in him, and how that unselfish soul of his lives in her. Godiva is not an ordinary young lady of the period; but one doesn't want to see her change. Who is it that says—

'Being everything which now thou art,
Be nothing which thou art not?'

I will ask her this very day. The child's head is crammed with poetry."

Three women were waiting for him at Richmond, and each was prepared to welcome him in a fashion of her own. Henrietta would be all the more glad to see him because he did not interfere with the nap, which was a Christian privilege on Sunday afternoon. Charlotte adored her boy, and glowed with pleasure at the thought of a possible love-making. And Godiva Durleigh, full of shy happiness, was wondering why the May world was so glorious, and life had put on a new aspect altogether! She could not believe that Rex had anything to do with all this fresh beauty and brightness which seemed to gladden the universe. The weather, she said, was uncommonly beautiful, and it was a delight to bask in the sunshine.

She stood at a narrow slit of a window on the stairs, and looked down into the road, watching unseen for Rex. Richmond is generally noisy on a Sunday. Yet it has quiet nooks and by-ways into which excursionists do not penetrate, and the Kemples' house was in one of these undiscovered spots. Birds were stirring in the ivy that grew so thickly around all the windows, and Godiva, as she watched, listened vaguely to their little chirps and trills. Presently she saw the tall figure coming along, and

as Rex drew near he glanced up. Then
she drew back with a quick thrill of
shame, afraid that he might catch a
glimpse of her too soon. What would
the two aunts think if they suspected that
she was looking out for their nephew?

In her haste to go down and receive
him properly in the presence of the old
ladies, she turned the corner of the stairs
too quickly. Miss Charlotte, with quite
a jovial air about her, was opening the
hall door with words of welcome. Rex
was hurried in, questioned, and made
much of; but he was looking round for
another greeting. Lifting his eyes, he
saw Godiva standing above him, her face
delicately flushed, and a shy grace in
her attitude. Even Miss Charlotte was
struck, and glanced eagerly from the girl
to Rex. Had he, too, discovered how
charming she was?

Perhaps he had; but his grave face and dark-blue eyes seldom betrayed secrets. Godiva came down slowly, step by step, and held out her little hand very quietly. Then Miss Henrietta appeared at the drawing-room door, and asked plaintively if they were not ready for luncheon? She liked her meals, and could not bear to be kept waiting.

Although Aunt Susanna was a good housekeeper, and comforts were not neglected in Buckingham Street, Godiva could not help enjoying the sense of homeliness which came to her in this old-fashioned household. These maiden sisters had ways of their own which seemed to impart a delicate flavour to everything. Even Rex, remembering the dainty banquets at the rectory, could find no fault with the meals at Garden Lodge. And to-day he was conscious

of finding something that had always
been wanting in his grandfather's house
—a young woman's presence.   Godiva
did not say much, but her clear eyes
met his sometimes.   She had put on her
best gown—one of her favourite greys,
soft in material and very well made—
and wore a little cravat of creamy muslin
and lace.   A bunch of heliotrope was
fastened near her throat, and its perfume floated towards him as he came
within the circle of her happy girlish
influence.

Was she pretty?   He supposed not,
if you judged her face by any rules; and
yet, if a woman has a thoroughly sympathetic nature, and a gift of saying
things well, she can generally beguile a
man into thinking her pretty.

After luncheon he followed her into
the garden, and found a curious, dreamy

delight in her society, and in the beauty of the old place. He noticed everything, and drew a keen pleasure out of everything—the blue of the sky, seen through a lattice of boughs; the gentle flutter of a myriad leaves; the soft colours of flowers. They went to the very bottom of the grounds, and then sat down on a bench to look at the river.

"I wonder if all those people are enjoying themselves as much as I am?" Rex said languidly, after a pause.

Godiva was watching the gay groups below them with a quiet smile—some walking along the towing-path, some darting by in boats, nearly all talking and laughing as if their lives had never known a care.

"I think it is all the pleasanter here because we can see them," she remarked. "I should not care for the kind of happiness that shuts out all sight and sound of humanity."

He gave her an amused glance, thinking how widely her notion of happiness differed from the rector's. His grandfather had always found enjoyment impossible unless there was a massive barrier between " other people " and himself. And then he was conscious that his own ideas had undergone a change. He had begun to find the sight of holiday-keepers quite endurable, and wondered whether he was slowly becoming Cockneyfied.

" I am discovering contentment where I least expected to find it," he said after another pause. " It's a great surprise to feel that I really take pleasure in this London life of mine. I had always wanted something very different, you know."

" Yes ; Miss Charlotte told me," she

answered, looking at him with a gentle air of interest. And then he reflected that he had talked about himself when he had seen her last, and now he was doing it again. Yet, undeterred by the consciousness of egotism, he went on: "Even Barnard's Inn has an attraction for me now. If Dickens could hear me say so, he would think that I was developing an unwholesome sympathy with mouldiness and mustiness. But— although new places have their advantages—it isn't a bad thing to live in some old corner full of memories."

"I know. One is never lonely when one has a few harmless ghosts for company," said Godiva.

He smiled, recalling his morning musings.

"I encourage the ghosts," he admitted. "Sometimes I summon Peter Woulfe to reappear, and tell me if he has found out all he wanted to know. You must come and look at his chambers one of these days. I don't think there have been many changes since he lived in them."

"He was one of the failures," Godiva said thoughtfully. "But he always said he should have discovered the elixir if he had set about his task in a holier spirit. I wonder if there is just a gleam of truth in that fancy of his? My father says you cannot achieve any great good until you have prepared yourself for the effort by utter self-renunciation. Dear father—some people say that the philanthropist is as wild a dreamer as the alchemist!"

The next instant he saw a look of sorrow in her eyes.

"Never mind what people say," he entreated. "Every strong endeavour to improve the world is sure to awaken a clamour of derision. And the man who tries hard always accomplishes something, even if he falls short of his purpose. We should be badly off indeed if we had no enthusiasts among us."

"If they would only give him more help!" The words came with a little sigh. "The paper doesn't succeed, you see."

If Rex had spoken out his thoughts he would have owned that he, for one, did not desire the success of that paper. But he would not tell Godiva that it was not as an editor that her father shone; he only said the first comforting words that occurred to him.

"Don't fret about the paper, Miss Durleigh. Your father has done more by his life than most men can accomplish with their pens. And I think we are over-deluged with printed matter now-adays. There are lots of people who revere the name of Morris Durleigh, although they have never read a line of the *Champion*."

The shadow passed away from her face, and she smiled at him gratefully.

" Some of his friends are hard on him for my sake," she said. " But they don't understand how happy I am, Mr. Long-worthy. Mamma was an invalid for a long time, and our pretty home in Kent was often sad. It was good for me to be moved into Buckingham Street, and taken care of by Aunt Susanna. One can make a home in lodgings just as well as in a villa. I don't want any changes; I should like to be always with my father in the dear old Strand. People talk, and judge one's life from their own standpoint; but they can't get a glimpse of the inner world in which one really lives."

Again did Rex keep his thoughts to himself. He did indeed admire Morris Durleigh from the bottom of his heart, but he could not feel that the father was doing justice to his child. Morris had brought Godiva up in a place which is supposed to be unfavourable to a girl's growth and culture. Very few of those advantages which she ought to have had were given to her. Even Miss Henrietta, who seldom concerned herself with other people's affairs, had said that Godiva Durleigh ought to have lived in a different kind of home.

And Rex agreed with Aunt Henrietta, conscious that his early notions of a girl's life and surroundings could never change. He did not know that a good deal of the old Longworthy pride was clinging to him still. The Longworthys had never cared to gather a flower unless they approved of the soil from which it had sprung. They might praise its sweetness, but the earth which had nourished the blossom was of more importance than the blossom itself. Rex found himself suddenly wishing that Godiva had been less contented with her lot.

"I wish," he said, breaking the brief silence in a low voice, "that your outer world was better fitted to contain the inner world of which you speak."

She turned, with a slight start and a vague look of troubled wonder in her glance.

"Oh, you are blaming my father in your mind," she cried. "I was afraid that you would."

"No," he said eagerly, "you must not have such fancies. But you are so happy in this pretty old garden, that one likes to think of you in a sheltered home. It seems as if you had no business to live in an ugly street where never a flower can grow."

But she was only half satisfied with his words, and had begun to say something in defence of her beloved street, when a loud scream came up from the path below the terrace.

In an instant Rex was on his feet, and had leaped right over the side of the terrace on to the path below. A moment afterwards he was in the river, striking out towards something that sank and vanished before he could get near it. Godiva stood up, dumb, with clasped hands and straining eyes. But the people on the towing-path were anything but dumb. They were shouting and gesticulating wildly, and the loud clamour of their voices bewildered the girl's brain. She could only stand there waiting, her hair pushed back from her white face.

"Ah, he's got hold of it!" cried a woman's voice shriller than the rest. Rex had clutched a little heap of clothes which had reappeared on the surface of the water; and presently, amid shouts and confused murmurs, he brought his dripping bundle safe to land.

Then Godiva collected her senses and remembered the steps that led down to the side-door. She flew to the door and unbolted it.

"The child is unconscious," panted Rex, hurrying up the steps with his burden. "Godiva, the little thing fell out of a boat. Its mother will be here presently, and you must bring her into the house."

He rushed away with his load, running

up the garden at a frantic pace. And Godiva stood watching two young men rowing towards the landing with a distracted woman in their boat.

A few minutes later she was conducting the frightened young mother along the path to the house, and trying to soothe her as they went.

"We have sent for a doctor," said Miss Charlotte, meeting them in the hall; "but cook has got the child, and says it will come back to life!"

CHAPTER X.

"HOW MANY SIMPLE WAYS THERE ARE TO BLESS."

AND cook was right; the child did come back to life, and was recovering itself when the doctor arrived. The young mother, pallid and helpless, clung to Godiva, and could hardly believe that her little girl was really restored to her. The Kemples drew a deep breath of relief when the men took the pair away in a cab. Henrietta was kind at heart, but hated anything in the shape of a scene; and Charlotte was always anxious on her sister's account.

"Henrietta can't bear excitement," she explained. "You see, Godiva, you are quite used to having things happen. Young people like adventures and startling incidents. I don't think Rex minded jumping into the river with all his clothes on. How brave he is, dear boy!"

But when all emotion had subsided it was discovered that Rex was in an awkward position. His own clothes were unfit for immediate use, and he was ringing bells upstairs, and sending peremptory messages to his aunts to get him something to wear. It was cook who came to the rescue when the ladies were at their wits' end.

"There's the old gentleman across the road," she suggested. "He must have a lot of clothes, surely, and he never goes beyond his garden. He's tall, too; much about Mr. Longworthy's height if he didn't stoop."

The sisters demurred. They had never asked favours of neighbours, and did not want to break their rules. And then the bell upstairs gave another loud peal; and Joy was hastily dispatched to old Mr. Romilly.

She came back with her arms full of garments. A little later Rex appeared in the drawing-room, looking like somebody in the "Arabian Nights," and challenging criticism fearlessly. A rich Oriental dressing-gown, with a silken girdle, draped him from neck to foot; and Miss Charlotte at once committed the imprudence of openly admiring him. Henrietta looked grave, and sank back in her chair with a little sigh which recalled her sister to a sense of propriety.

If the truth must be told there was

something in Henrietta's gentle depression which damped the spirits of the rest. She confided to Charlotte afterwards that she had thought Rex's costume almost indecent. He ought to have shut himself up in a room alone if he had to be dressed like that. It was really dreadful to see him talking to Godiva in a dressing-gown. But in Godiva's eyes the unusual costume had a strange charm. It reminded her of his heroic action. Her strong idealism had magnified Rex's simple exploit into a magnificent deed.

She had, however, too much natural modesty and grace to make any display of hero-worship. It was expressed only in a certain quietness of speech and thoughtfulness of look; but Rex understood that he had made an impression, and did not regret his cold bath. It was very pleasant to know that a pair of grey

eyes were looking at him with furtive
devotion. He had been cheaply turned
into a hero, it was true; but he saw no
reason why he should not wear the laurel
that had been so painlessly won.

Later on in his life he looked back on
the Rex of that evening with a bitter
contempt. He was accepting everybody's affection as easily and naturally
as if it had been a gift of summer flowers.
But afterwards, when the winter of his
days set in, he remembered all the rare
sweetness of that simple love, and wondered why it had been so lightly prized.

Before they went to bed, Miss Henrietta had forgiven him for being so
comfortable and unembarrassed in the
dressing-gown. She had asked Godiva
to play some hymn-tunes, and they all
sang hymns in the evening stillness.
Godiva was not a fine singer, but her

voice was sweet and true, and harmon-
ized with the quiet mood of her hearers.
The little drawing-room was more homelike than it had ever been before—more
homelike even than any of those beautiful old rooms in the rectory which Rex
had once loved so well.

It is an important moment in a young
man's life when he gets his first glimpse
of a possible home; and that moment
came to Rex Longworthy in the little
Richmond house on this Sunday evening. Such moments come to all men's
lives, and are swept away, often enough,
by a tide of new experiences and
anxieties; yet they seldom pass without
leaving some faint memory behind.

There is always something sacred in
the first yearning of a man for his Eden.
It seems such an easy happiness to attain
—just a common kind of bliss that only

needs a little nook to contain it—just a nest where two may sing the old song together, and be alone with their joy. Ah, if one could only build that nest as the swallows build theirs, with little bits of stick and clay, how soon one could make a home! But poor human lovers must needs encumber themselves with bricks and mortar, tables and chairs, before they can begin that sweet wedded life which they pine for. There are too many " social wants that sin against the strength of youth."

I wonder whether we should hear less about marriage as a failure if two persons who fancy each other could fly straight away together to the nearest parson, and be tied up without any fuss? While the settlements are drawn out, and the house is being furnished, and the trousseau made, there is time for the dew to dry.

Love, like a field - flower, should be gathered in the first freshness of its morning. I once heard a man say, with evident sincerity, that it was an easy thing to fall in love, and a difficult thing to get married.

But on the other hand there are those who warn us against "raw haste," and speak of the slow sweet growth of an affection that strikes its roots deep into the soil of life. They tell us that "patience must have her perfect work" before the reality of love is duly proved. All the voices have reason in them; but their tones clash sometimes, and leave us, too often, with the confused din of many doubts murmuring in our ears.

With Godiva near, Rex was floated along by waves of pleasant sensation which made life easy. There were no wild heart-throbs, no passionate desires;

but a calm satisfaction deepened with every hour of their intercourse. The light faded slowly; Miss Charlotte sat by the window, and silently repeated scraps of sentimental poetry to herself. Miss Henrietta, growing sleepy, was lulled by a gentle sound of young voices, and closed her eyes in peace.

"Good night," said Rex, with a lingering hand-clasp. "This has been a perfect day. I shall go back to Barnard's Inn with May perfumes lingering about me. Won't you ask your father to spare you for another Sunday, Miss Durleigh?"

"No; I can't ask him that." Godiva's cheeks flushed faintly. "He would miss me so—all the more because he wouldn't say a word."

"But his mind is always full of plans. Do you think he has leisure to miss any one?"

Her face had been slightly averted, but now she turned it towards him.

"Nothing ever makes him forget *me*," she answered confidently. "If I am not near he is always conscious of a sense of loss, although he doesn't talk of it. Aunt Susanna is good, but she can't fill my place."

"That I can believe," he said, with an intent look.

The girl went away to her room, unable to understand her own unreasonable happiness. What reason was there for this strange delight in life? She had spent a happy time with a new friend who seemed to like her, that was all. At twenty Godiva was more ignorant than most girls; she had never had a lover.

One or two leading novelists had come to see her father sometimes; and she had read love-scenes, written by these very men, which had thrilled her from head to foot. But the men themselves had seemed to her to be the most prosaic creatures in existence. They created heroes; they idealized men and women, and presented them to the reader as human beings touched with divine light. The creations were exquisite, but the creator was of the earth, earthy to the last degree. This was Godiva's estimate of her father's friends; but Morris liked the genial, hearty men, and found help and comfort in their frank sympathy.

As she sat that night in her room, and looked out through a frame of leaves into the bright moonlight, she felt that one of her dreamed-of men had stepped out of a novel, and stood in flesh and blood beside her. Rex was so heroic, she thought. All his gentleness to his two aunts, all his grave courtesy to herself, rose up before her mind and strengthened the spell of fascination. For a little while even her father was forgotten. Leaves quivered and rustled in the low breeze; clouds drifted near the moon and caught her silver light; flowers sent up their faint, sweet breath; and Godiva leant out, dreaming, into the night air.

Monday morning dawned, a sweet rain-washed morning, and Rex, when he came downstairs, found Godiva alone in the breakfast-room.

"I am to see that you have a good breakfast," she said. "Miss Henrietta feels a little shattered, and Miss Charlotte is waiting upon her upstairs. The kindest thing you can do this morning is to be hungry. If you are not hungry they will lay the blame of your bad appetite on me."

" You shan't be blamed for any sins of mine," he answered, watching her stead-fastly as she took a seat at the table, and poured out his coffee.

The morning light, which visited the back of the house, made its way into the cosy room through a maze of tendrils and ivy leaves that cast light shadows on Godiva's gown. She did not eat much, and rarely looked up without meeting his eyes.

Rex was not accustomed to receive the little housewifely attentions of a young woman, and this experience was new and strange and very sweet. His mother had died in his childhood, he had never had a sister, at the rectory his grand-father had always presided at meals; and his life at Barnard's Inn had only been varied by his visits to Garden Lodge. To find himself sitting alone with a girl, accepting pretty little services from her hands, was something pleasant and bewildering.

The oddest part of the matter was its perfect naturalness ; it was as if his past life had been a dream, and he had suddenly awakened to a happy reality. It seemed as if they two ought to have been sitting at one table for years, and should be looking forward to sitting so together till the end of their days.

All the trivial words they spoke were invested with a curious importance ; common things became significant ; Charlotte's robin, hopping on the window-sill, was felt to be a sharer of their joy, and a harbinger of good. Henrietta's cat, trained to affect a total disregard of birds, came purring round them so loudly that the sleepy contented sound filled up every pause in the talk. These living soulless creatures seemed to divine their happiness, and be glad of it in a fashion of their own.

"I shall find my way to Buckingham Street," he said, when they were parting. "You are going back soon?"

"To-morrow," she replied.

"Going back to all the delights of the Strand, and your dear old Water-gate! Well, I shall come and try to discover the attractions of that part for myself, if you will let me."

"Yes," she answered, "I will let you come."

CHAPTER XI.

THE cool sweetness of May gave place to a hot June, and Rex, when he went to see the Durleighs, always wondered how any one could spend a summer in the Strand. Yet Godiva, with her gentle enthusiasm about the nooks and by-ways of the place, almost overcame his dislike to her surroundings. And Morris, with his intense eagerness, his manifold plans and aspirations, awakened the young man's warmest sympathies.

Godiva had the art of dressing well, but she had very little money to spend

on her gowns. Sometimes when she had
made up her mind to have a new costume
there was a case of pressing need; a
child was destitute and must be clothed
and fed; and at the mere suggestion of
distress she forgot her own small wants
and flew to the help of the needy. It
seemed to her the most natural thing in
the world to care for the children of the
poor.

"There is so little that one can do for
grown-up people," Morris used to say.
"But there is everything to be done for
the children. If we have any hope of a
better future for humanity it must come
through them. It is to them that we
must look for our harvest—'the harvest-
time of love.'"

"You must have long patience if you
wait till that harvest comes. It won't
be in your life," said Rex thoughtfully.

"No," Morris answered; "I have never dreamt of being more than a sower of seed. But I have always felt that even this is worth living for."

"Yet a sower's is a kind of unfinished, disappointing life," Rex said. "I could not stand it."

"I used to think so," Morris spoke in a very quiet voice; "but now I am sure that we must live as close to our ideal life as we can if we would escape the worst kind of disappointment. To some of us, perhaps, there is a sweetness in the sense of failure; it is a promise that God will complete the work that we cannot finish. Victor Hugo has said that success is a hideous thing. I will not go as far as that, yet there is truth in the harsh saying."

There was a silence. Rex remembered afterwards how quickly the last of the summer day seemed to fade that evening. Then Morris spoke again.

"Perhaps at the very last the work may not look as unfinished as it does now. We may even have a sense of completeness given us at the end. St. Paul must have had to leave many things undone, and yet he could say at the close, 'I have fought a good fight, I have *finished* my course, I have kept the faith.'"

A few seconds of intense quietness followed these words. Then Godiva stirred with a little quick breath, and Morris rose from his seat.

"Father," she pleaded, "don't go out again this evening; it is growing quite late. Why not take some rest? You have been working so hard!"

"I must go," he answered. "I promised to see Lizzy Hammond at half-past nine. At that time the man will be out of the way, and there will be a chance of peace. She says that she must hear something of her child or go mad; and she wants to talk to me about little Ted."

" Shall you send little Ted to the Refuge, too ? " Godiva asked.

" He is almost too old; but something must be done. Drink has turned Hammond into a perfect fiend. Poor Lizzy is pining after her baby girl."

" Then the baby is taken from her ? " said Rex.

" Yes; she gave it to us just to save its life. Hammond would have dashed its brains out if it had been left in its mother's care. Poor Lizzy is pining after the little thing. Poor Lizzy! she was a mother at sixteen, and she is but a girl still."

So Morris turned to go his way. But

before he could reach the door Godiva sprang after him.

"Kiss me, father," she cried, lifting up her face to his.

He gazed at her steadily for an instant, as if he were plunged in deep thought. Then his eyes brightened, although he looked aged and worn.

"My dear," he said, "my only dear child!" He drew her into his arms, and kissed her tenderly. The door closed, and she came slowly back to the parlour, where Rex was sitting in the lamplight. She sat down opposite to him, and, resting her elbows on the table, dropped her forehead upon her hands.

"I am afraid you are very tired," he said gently. "It has been a hot day; the weather is exhausting, and you need change and fresh air."

She looked up quickly with a faint smile.

"No," she answered; "not exactly tired, but burdened with a weight of feeling. When father carries such a heavy load some of it must rest on me."

"It is too much for him and for you," Rex exclaimed.

"But I would not have it otherwise," she said in a low sweet voice. "We understand each other—father and I."

Rex made a slight movement of impatience, but instantly grew quiet again.

"I have wondered sometimes whether you have any young relatives?" he said after a pause. "Girls of your own age, you know. It would be nice to get out of London and stay with them for a little while, wouldn't it?"

"Oh no; I shouldn't like it at all!" she replied. "I have some first cousins —three girls. They are the daughters of father's only brother, a lawyer, who lives

in Silversea. My father was to have
been a lawyer, but he gave up the
idea."

" Have you ever seen those cousins ? "
Rex asked.

" Only once." Godiva laughed a little,
and pretended to shudder. " They were
staying at the Langham Hotel, and I
called on them. I dare say the interview
was as unpleasant to them as to me.
We tried to make conversation and
utterly failed. Disapproval was written
in every line of their faces."

" But why should they disapprove of
you ? " Rex inquired.

" Because I am father's daughter."
She flushed as she spoke. " They are
ashamed of being connected with him ;
they hate his opinions, and they don't
see the beauty of his life."

" Perhaps if they knew you better,"

suggested Rex, "they would learn to love him for your sake."

Her tender heart beat with a quick delight, but she answered firmly—

"That wouldn't satisfy me. They must learn to love him for his own sake, and learn to realize all the good that he is doing, before I can be their friend."

"You are wonderfully loyal," he said.

"Is loyalty an uncommon quality?" she asked. "I think not. Disloyalty seems to me to be much more difficult than loyalty."

Their talk drifted away, after a time, from the theme of Godiva's cousins. Rex saw that she did not care to speak of them, and found that she really had very little knowledge of them. Then they chatted about the books they had read, the pictures they had seen, the poems that lingered longest in their memories. At last the clock struck ten; and Aunt Susanna, who had been busy elsewhere, came suddenly into the room. As she entered Rex got up to go.

" I have stayed an unconscionable time," he said.

" No," she answered; "I am glad you have stayed, Mr. Longworthy. It would have been lonely for Godiva if you hadn't been here. I thought Mr. Durleigh would have come home earlier."

"I wish he would come!" Godiva exclaimed. " Hark!" ·

There was a rattle of wheels in the narrow street, and a cab stopped at the door.

Rex never knew why he was suddenly possessed with the conviction that something had happened; yet it was certain that as he stood in the little parlour, looking steadfastly into Godiva's eager face, he was bracing himself to meet a coming shock.

Miss Hayward went to the hall-door and opened it, and Rex stood looking into the entry over Godiva's head. He saw the elder woman start and put her hand up to her forehead; and then, with a very gentle movement, he swept Godiva aside.

"Some one is hurt," said Aunt Susanna in a terrified whisper.

They were bringing Morris Durleigh back to the house he had left scarcely two hours ago, and they carried him gently across the threshold. Rex helped to support the helpless figure in his strong young arms, and laid him down tenderly on the sofa. The men who had brought him were rough fellows who knew him, and knew also where he lived. It had all happened close by, in one of

those dark alleys which teem with life
and its mysteries of suffering and sin.
And it was Hammond who had struck the
blow—mad Hammond, drunken Hammond!—whose baby Morris Durleigh had
rescued from destruction.

So this follower of the Good Shepherd
had given his life for the sheep, as his
Master had done before him.

They thought at first that he might
be spared to them; but the doctor, who
came at Rex's summons, saw that there
was no hope. He revived once, and once
only, and recognized his daughter's face
bending over him.

"I have saved some of the people's
children," he said in a faint voice. "I
leave my child to God."

They did not move him from the couch
where he had often lain in his brief
intervals of rest. There was only a short

period of pain and delirium, and then the perfect quietness of eternal peace.

Thus died in the prime of manhood, and by a violent death, a man whose whole life had been laid as a sacrifice upon the altar of humanity. He had trodden a rough path, made rougher than it need have been by his own blunders, but planted nevertheless with sweeter flowers than ever grow in the world's common way. He had loved God's whispered " Well done " better than men's shouts of acclamation; and he had learnt that the essence of Christ's meaning is found in many warring sects, and His love in many hearts whose creeds are always clashing against each other.

Some days afterwards, when those who had loved him were turning over his papers, they came upon certain words written when he had undertaken the editorship of the unsuccessful journal :—

"My duty as an Editor will be to know all men, to use everything, and to fear nothing—that is the ideal. To help all good causes, to smite with the thunderbolt of God all baseness, false-hood, devilishness ; to add fresh hope to every good man or woman working in every good cause, to be the dread of every evil-doer. I ought, to reproduce in my paper the ideal of a God : the helper of those who have no helper, the hope of the oppressed, the cloudy pillar by day, the fiery cloud by night. I ought to be the revealer of the secrets of God, the director of the steps of His people, the centre of a beneficent influence flow-ing out over the whole world. A real paper ought to be the strengthener of all good tendencies ; a bulwark against encroaching wrong ; the enlightener of

all men as to the good in their neighbours, and as to the wrongs which remain
unremoved ; the great tribune of the
poor, the conscience of the rich ; the
brooding influence which will quicken
into activity all good aspirations and
spur into unrest all lethargic souls ; the
constant presentation of a sublime ideal,
side by side with an intensely practical
guidance as to every immediate step to
be taken towards its attainment ; a
medium of intercommunication between
all departments of human activity ; a
source of consolation and inspiration to
all the better longings of the human heart.
In short, I ought to make my paper like
Longfellow's ' Universal Church '—

> ' As lofty as the love of God,
>   And wide as the wants of man.'

"To that I am called. . . . I may do
none of these things.   Others may be

called to do the work which I see needs
to be done. So be it. I am well content, so the work be done. But who
can hear the wail of misery that runs
ceaselessly from the great aching heart
of man! Who can see the frightful seeth-
ing gulf of wretchedness, the sulphurous
hell in which whole generations welter,
without wishing to multiply a thousand-
fold the agencies by which their fires
can be quenched, and their feet planted
on the rock; that, in short, Thy king-
dom may come on earth even as in
heaven, without crying, 'Here am I;
send me!' And I believe that God has
called me and anointed me unto this
mission. And I shall be not only a
centre of life and love and power in my
own paper, but the whole ideal of news-
papers will be so raised that my own
paper will be but as one among many.
I am content if it be done by others."

CHAPTER XII.

DAYS OF HEALING.

THE cruel blow that had fallen upon Godiva left her prostrate for many weary days. While she lay, half-stupefied with grief, in her little room at the top of the house, she knew very little of what was going on downstairs. The doctor said she had narrowly escaped a nervous fever, and insisted on perfect quietness.

The trial most dreaded by her friends was the day of her coming down into the world again—that world in which there was such a terrible void now.

Aunt Susanna and Charlotte Kemple

had devised a plan for her good, and Rex was at hand to help them in carrying out their scheme.

The summer evening was soft and bright when they brought her down. Rex was standing, tall and straight, at the foot of the stairs, and a cab was waiting at the open door. She looked up languidly into his face, and said that Aunty was going to take her for a drive.

"Miss Hayward is not going," Rex answered, taking the slender little hand and drawing it through his arm. "You must trust yourself to Aunt Charlotte and me. Godiva, everything is arranged, and you are to stay at Richmond till you get strong."

"Oh no; let me stay here," she pleaded feebly. "There is so much to think of; so many things to be done."

"But you are not fit to do anything

yet," said Rex, with gentle firmness. "Trust to us, Godiva; we will manage better for you than you can for yourself."

He led her out of the familiar door, and, half lifting her into the cab, placed her by Miss Charlotte's side. Then he gave a quick direction to the driver, and got in after her.

Godiva saw nothing during that short drive to Waterloo Railway Station. She kept her eyes shut, and the tears forced their way between the closed lids; yet she was conscious of the clasp of Miss Charlotte's arm, and felt a vague sense of comfort and protection. And then came the little journey to Richmond, the clear warm tints of the sky at sunset, the cool green of trees and fields, and the gleam of the shining river. At the door of Garden Lodge stood Joy awaiting her coming.

As the eyes of these two girls met
they both remembered their first meeting
on a winter day gone by. Then it was
Godiva who had stood, full of gladness,
on the threshold to welcome the forlorn
wanderer in. Now it was Joy's turn to
bind up the broken heart, and strengthen
the weak hands held out to her in mute
entreaty for help. At this desolate
moment of her life no one, perhaps,
could have comforted Godiva so well as
the woman who owed peace and safety
to him who was gone.

The Kemples wisely left her in Joy's
care that night. It was strange to find
herself lying in a little bed with white
curtains, and feeling the scented breath
of the summer night coming softly
through the open window. Joy moved
about noiselessly, and at last sat down
in a chair by the bedside. She sat thus,

holding Godiva's hand until the sick girl slept.

The waking, soon after daybreak, was bewildering. Godiva's head was still weak from recent illness, and she collected her thoughts slowly; yet, by-and-by, lying in her white nest, she tasted the sweetness of being away from the scene of her sorrow.

The room in which she lay had a charming quaintness which pleased her eyes, and carried her mind off into a far-away past which did not belong to her own life. The looking-glass, in its carved frame, stood on a slender-legged table in company with a large pin-cushion, which looked as if it had been whipped up into a foam of muslin frills. In a corner there was a triangular washing-stand with an enchanting ewer and basin of straw-coloured china. The pitcher was high, and wrought all over with a basket-work pattern; and spout and handle were composed of roses, massed together with green leaves. The basin, shallow and broad, had a garland of roses all round the brim. Miss Charlotte had remembered how her own eyes had been gladdened, in her youth, by this gay ware, and she had got out the things and set them in Godiva's room. Godiva was fanciful, she said, and would like to imagine that the water smelt of the roses.

Other roses, short-lived but far sweeter, were brought to her bedside in the early morning. They made their appearance with Joy and a cup of cocoa.

"Mr. Longworthy gathered them for you, miss," said Joy, putting them down gently on the coverlet. "He was out in the garden before breakfast with Miss Charlotte's best scissors."

"The poor scissors!" Godiva murmured.

"Yes, miss; he took them out of her work-basket without leave. He wanted you to have the flowers as soon as you were awake. You know, miss, he had to go off early to business."

"He is very kind." Godiva bent her pale face over the roses, and Joy watched her with quiet satisfaction. "I suppose he won't come back this evening?"

"No, miss, not till Saturday. But this is Thursday." There was a great deal of meaning conveyed in those four simple words. Joy wanted Godiva to feel that only to-day and to-morrow stood between Rex's next visit to Garden Lodge; and Godiva, crushed and shattered as she was, had enough vitality left in her to thrill with gladness.

She was young, and she and Rex had

glided swiftly and easily into that close intimacy which, between two young people, is the beginning of union. He had known and valued her father; he had stood by when Morris Durleigh drew his last breath. In Godiva's heart Rex was glorified by the solemn light of that great sorrow; she could not think of her grief without a thought of him.

The man who appears at any great crisis of a woman's life is sure to influence her afterwards. Rex had supported her in her hour of anguish; he had been calm and strong when others had lost courage; he seemed to possess all the attributes of a true hero. And there was a rare gentleness combined with his strength, and a tender consideration for her tastes and likings—else why had this bunch of roses found its way to her bedside?

When she came downstairs, looking very frail and white, there was a cheerfulness in her face which the Kemples had hardly expected to see. They plucked up spirit enough to tell her that a dressmaker was coming to make her some black gowns, and Godiva owned sadly that she had felt too ill to think about mourning.

"Your aunt left the matter to us, my dear," said Henrietta, gently. "We shall give you as little trouble as possible. But you must have good clothes, nicely made. A girl cannot be too particular on that point."

"Oh, it doesn't matter how the things are made!" Godiva sighed.

"Excuse me, my dear, but it *does* matter." Miss Henrietta was mild, but positive. "You do not know where you will have to wear your clothes; you may be going to new scenes, among new people, and you must make a good impression."

"New scenes?" repeated Godiva, wearily. "When I leave Garden Lodge I am going back to Buckingham Street. Dear Miss Henrietta, there will be nothing new there, excepting—excepting the vacant place that will never be filled up in this world!"

Miss Charlotte got up, with tears twinkling in her sharp hazel eyes, and overturned a little table. Miss Henrietta was going to cry too, but when she saw the table fall she mildly reproved her sister.

"You are so impetuous, dear Charlotte," she said. "My poor nerves!"

Charlotte set the table on its treacherous little legs with an angry jerk. Why should a weakly bit of furniture come betwixt herself and her emotions ? Why should they concern themselves with this senseless thing when a human being was on the verge of heart-break? But Henrietta, she reflected, would worry over a dropped stitch in her knitting while heaven and earth were passing away around her. Henrietta would fret about a spot on her gown if the solid ground were crumbling to pieces beneath her feet.

Poor Godiva, undisturbed by the fall of the table, was crying quietly, and vaguely wondering why they were so fussy about her mourning? And then a swift flash of remembrance warmed her pale cheeks. Rex was one of those men who know what women wear, and can tell when they are well dressed. Perhaps the aunts—good creatures—were studying Rex's taste, and thinking how to please him.

She did not in the least suspect that they had something to say to her, and did not know how to say it. Once Henrietta began in a feeble way—

" It was a pity you could not see your uncle Hugh, my dear."

" Uncle Hugh ? " Godiva had almost forgotten his existence. " Oh yes ; he came to the—the funeral ; but I was upstairs, and hardly knew that he was in the house. Aunt Susanna said he was very nice and kind."

" Oh, very nice and kind," repeated Henrietta with unusual animation. " My brother has heard him exceedingly well spoken of. And Joseph's opinion may be safely relied upon."

" Yes, he was always grateful to my father," said Godiva, trying to take an interest in the subject, and say something kind about the relative of whom she knew so little. " He has never forgotten that my father lent him money when he wanted it very badly in the beginning of his business life. It was nice in Uncle Hugh not to forget the benefit, but I know his wife and daughters were angry that it should be remembered."

" My dear child, you must endeavour to encourage a charitable spirit," remarked Miss Henrietta, softly patting the girl's shoulder with her delicate mittened hand. " I am sure your cousins are very kindly disposed towards you. Miss Hayward said that they sent messages of sympathy which you were too ill to receive. You know, my love, that young people easily become friends; you will learn to like your relations when you know them better."

" But I shall never know them better." Godiva looked at her with a sad wonder.

"Of course I shall always be poor, and they are rich; their mother had a good deal of money, I believe, and Uncle Hugh has prospered. It is not likely that they will have anything to do with me."

Miss Henrietta's dove-like eyes appealed to her sister. But Charlotte saw that the time for making a certain revelation had not yet come. She got up a little fuss, declared that Godiva must be ready for beef-tea, suggested that she should sit in the garden in the afternoon sun, and wondered whether Rex would bring the Japanese umbrella which was to be fixed on the garden chair. Nothing more was said about the Durleighs at Silversea till the old ladies were alone at night.

"How are we ever to tell her?" inquired Henrietta, in a tone of gentle despair. " I had no idea it would be so difficult ! "

" We have both tried and failed," said Charlotte, " and we won't try any more. Rex must do it."

CHAPTER XIII.

WHAT REX HAD TO SAY.

SUNDAY afternoon had come round again, and Rex and Godiva were sitting under the cedar in the old garden. He was looking at her as she sat propped up with cushions in a large cane chair, and thinking what a slender thing she was, and how impossible it would be for a fragile girl to fight the battle of life.

But there was not any need for her to fight; fate was kind, and a comfortable home had opened its doors to receive her. There she might dwell in peace, and lay up stores of knowledge and experience, until—— Here Rex pulled himself up short, and smiled. He was very young, and was not quite certain that he had found his ideal woman ; yet there were not many doubts to trouble his mind.

But now he had to say something to Godiva which would not please her at all; the aunts had tried to say it and failed, and had left the task on his hands. He was not unwilling to undertake that task, although it was certainly a painful one. If she was to suffer, it was better for him to inflict the suffering than for any one else to do it. He understood the art of healing as others did not. He was sure of his own power to still her quivering nerves, and represent the future in bright colours to her sad eyes. Dear little Godiva—as he looked at her his heart gave a quick throb of tenderness.

"If one could but take her away from all her troubles!" he mused; and then she turned and met his gaze.

"Don't be vexed with me if I am stupid to-day," she said, with a wistful smile. "It is so beautifully calm here, that one sits and watches the lights and shadows in silence."

"Do you call it stupid to be silent," he asked. "I wish some people thought it stupid to talk, and then we should have a little more peace in a noisy world. No, Godiva; it does me good to see you at rest."

"The rest won't last very long, I'm afraid." She sighed slightly. "Rex, I must think about finding something to do, as soon as I get well."

"Oh, you are not to think about that," he answered. "And you are a long way from being well yet; there are a good many weeks of comfortable invalidism before you."

"No, no." She shook her head with a quiet air of resolution. "It isn't good for me to be petted and made lazy; I shall get so used to this sunny paradise that it will be all the harder to face a bleak world. Don't tempt me to stay here too long."

Rex smiled. He was heartily glad at that moment that there was to be no facing a bleak world for her. But he knew that she would not receive the announcement of her good fortune with any delight.

She had sunk back upon the cushions again, and was looking languidly at the golden lights slipping through twisted boughs upon turf and gravel. There was a sleepy droning of bees; tall lilies stood up, white and pure as angel sentinels

guarding a sacred Eden; marigolds
burned here and there like amber stars.
Godiva gazed at everything with thoughtful grey eyes; and Rex, swinging a bit
of stick with an affectation of careless-
ness, was studying her face intently.

"You want a complete change,
Godiva," he said at last. "It is good
for us all to be taken out of an old groove
and set in a new. If our positions in the
world were fixed and unalterable how
terrible life would be!"

"Perhaps it would," she murmured.
"And yet—who doesn't know the agony
of change?"

"My dear child, it is very natural that
you should find sadness in everything
just now. Godiva, I wish I could bear
your sorrow for you; but I cannot. I
can only tell you that I understand what
you feel. Oh, poor child, surely there

can't be much more suffering reserved for you! Your bright days are coming fast."

She turned to him with eyes full of earnest gratitude, confident in her young trustfulness, that he was a prophet, fore-telling certain bliss. He met her glance frankly and tenderly, for he had spoken in all sincerity; and yet if he could have looked into the future he would have seen that her bright days were still far off, and that some of her darkest hours would come through him.

"Yes, you must believe in the happy times that are drawing near, even if they don't seem happy just at first," he went on. "Godiva, haven't you had enough of streets and houses and smoke? Shouldn't you like to live by the sea?"

"The sea? I have never thought

about it," she replied, with a puzzled look. "You know that my only home is with Aunt Susanna."

"But another home is open to you," he said impressively, "and it was your father's wish that you should go and live in it. Godiva, I see that you don't understand. He did not hint to you that he desired you to live at Silversea?"

"At Silversea? No, Rex," she faltered, growing very pale. "I never heard him speak of such a thing."

"But he thought of it and spoke of it," Rex continued, with quiet earnestness. "And 'just before he was called away from us he had a long talk with his friend Salterne."

"With Mr. Salterne?" Godiva flushed faintly, and there was a slight touch of scorn in her tone. "Oh yes, he was always lecturing father and advising him to do good sensible things! But his words could have had no influence."

"They had an influence. Dear Godiva," —he laid his hand softly upon hers—"you must not undervalue a good friend because he is a little prosaic and commonplace. I dare say Salterne often bored your father very much, but his counsel was followed after all."

Godiva had a broad brow, over which the curly hair grew low, and Rex had learnt to watch a slight knitting of the forehead which gave a tender troubled look to the whole face. It was a look which said plainly that she wanted to do right, even if right-doing was a terribly hard thing. After a moment's pause she turned towards him appealingly, and spoke with a sad tremor in her voice.

"You have to tell me something," she said. "It has not been told sooner because I wasn't strong enough to bear any agitation. But I see—yes, I do see now—why your aunts have been so particular about my black gowns. Oh, Rex, did father really say that I must go to Silversea?"

"Godiva, you know how I hate to pain you," he began, still keeping his hand on hers. "Only I feel that the thing which looks like a trouble will prove to be a blessing. Now I must speak plainly, and you will try to believe that all is arranged for the best. As I was saying just now, John Salterne's words had an influence, and your father wrote to your uncle, and said——"

"Yes, Rex?"

"Said that if ever you were left an orphan he wished his brother to take your father's place. And Hugh Durleigh readily promised to do this. He is more than willing, Godiva, to fulfil that promise now."

She leaned forward a little, and tried to draw her hand from his clasp; but he would not let it go. Slight as she looked, there was such an intensity of determination in her face that its expression startled him.

"Rex," she asked suddenly, "I have a little money, haven't I?"

"Yes," he said with great gentleness. "John Salterne is taking care of it for you, and the interest which you are to receive will suffice to pay for your dress when you live with your uncle. You must not think that you will depend on him for everything."

A change had taken place in her manner; the nervous wistfulness was gone. There was a sort of deadly stillness about her now which disquieted

Rex, and told him that the worst part of the struggle was coming.

"I won't go to Silversea," she said. "I will live with Aunt Susanna, and make the money go as far as it can. My attic is good enough for me; I don't want luxuries and fine clothes. I want to live in the dear old street, and see the great crowds and work among them. I can't give up the People's Garden, and the people——"

She stopped short. Her voice had broken, and she turned her pale face away from Rex.

He gave her hand an earnest pressure.

"Dear Godiva," he said, "I knew it would be hard. But you will have to go."

She drew a long breath, and for a moment they looked into each other's eyes. Hers were wild and miserable.

"Oh, I can't bear it," she cried. "Rex, I had a plan which I meant to keep a secret. My plan was to write stories. I don't think I am a genius; but father used to say that talent sometimes got better paid than genius, and I believe I have a little talent."

"And I believe you have a great deal," he replied. "But it will not do to depend upon it. Think of the thousands who try literature and fail! Your father would not have his daughter exposed to the disappointments of such a life as you dream of. It would not be good for you, poor child; it would harden you."

"Don't you think that it would harden me more to live with uncongenial people?" she asked bitterly.

"No," he answered. "You may find unexpected sympathies among them.

Few people are absolutely unendurable. Only we mustn't expect too much; we must not begin by expecting perfect harmony; it is best even to be prepared for a jarring note or two. But anyhow if we are sensible we can manage to get on."

"Manage to get on! That is not my idea of living," she said with quiet scorn. "And it was not my father's idea at all. Oh, Rex," the sweet voice trembled with passionate pain, "do you think father really meant me to go to Uncle Hugh? Isn't it a mistake?"

"It is not a mistake; you shall read your father's letter to your uncle," he replied, watching her very closely. "And, indeed, it will be the best thing for you—the very best thing. You will be thoroughly rested before you go, and then you will see everything in a new light. I dare say my words sound very cold and tame, poor child; but I am feeling deeply with you."

"Yes," she returned, without looking at him, "I am sure that you do feel. But you are mistaken in saying that I shall ever see this matter in a new light. To me it will always look just as it does now. And father never knew that I did not like the Durleigh girls. Oh, if I could only see him for one moment, and tell him how miserable I am!"

She threw up her hands with a quick, despairing gesture that went to Rex's heart. He got up, flung his bit of stick upon the grass, and looked away into space.

"Listen, Godiva," he said after a brief silence. "I, too, have had to choose the path I hated to tread. I had to turn my back upon the soldier's life that I had dreamed of from my childhood. I had to force my mind into a new channel, and learn to be a man of business. Do you think that your case is harder than mine?"

She did not speak, but looked at him anxiously, waiting to hear more.

"If I had become a soldier," he went on, "I must have borrowed the necessary funds from an old man whose means were not large. I knew he would have helped me at any cost; but I wasn't quite such a cur as to let him do it. And so I just accepted my fate."

"And you don't regret your decision?" she asked with suppressed eagerness.

"No; I should do the same again if it had to be done. Mind, I don't say that I've forgotten the old dream. It looks just as fair as ever, even now. Sometimes I seem to see a ring of friendly faces round the barrack fire; sometimes I am haunted by the fife and drum; and the wandering soldier's life, rough and cheery, often strikes me as being the most desirable life in the world."

"You did right to give it up," said Godiva. "But my case isn't quite the same. I might give all my money to Aunt Susanna, and——"

"Forgive me," he broke in, sitting down by her side again, "but you girls don't understand money matters. How should you? Again I say forgive me when I tell you that the interest of your money is not sufficient to cover all your expenses. Dear Godiva, you would not burden Miss Hayward; she would bear the burden willingly enough, and rejoice under it; but she is poor."

She sprang up from her seat among

the cushions, and stood before him for the instant a new creature, very fragile, and yet stronger than he had thought it possible she could be, her large grey eyes bright with intense feeling, a spot of colour burning on each pale cheek.

"You need not say another word," she said in a clear sweet voice. "Oh, how good it is for people to be told a plain downright truth! And how dense I have been! Why did I not know everything instinctively, and spare you the pain of speaking out? Rex, I will not trouble any one again with my stupid opposition. I will go to Silversea, and try to be as agreeable and conventional as I can. Let me have time to practise before I depart, because I foresee that I shall require a great deal of polishing!"

She ended her speech with a brave little laugh, which was not unmusical, although it had not much mirth in it. And then all her fictitious strength suddenly deserted her; the colour died out of her cheeks and the light out of her eyes.

"I soon get tired now," she said faintly. Rex put his arm round the slight figure and drew it back into its resting-place.

There was enough to pity in her. She saw pain and tender compassion in the deep blue eyes that looked into hers; but she did not know how white and worn she was. Only once a sob broke from her as she clung to the cushions in a helpless way like a child.

"Oh, Godiva," he said, "I wish, with all my heart, that I could have spared you this!"

"You have been good to me," she answered. "You said a hard thing softly and kindly. I will do as well as I can. I will try to be all that my father's daughter ought to be. But don't wonder at my weakness now."

"Indeed," he said, "I am wondering at your strength."

For a few seconds there was stillness —such stillness as the rustle of many leaves and the murmur of small winged things only seem to deepen. When Rex spoke again his voice was so low and sweet that it seemed to come from far away.

"Godiva," he said, "is there any need for all this terrible suffering? You feel that you are going into exile; true, but exile does not always mean perpetual banishment. In a year or two you may come back to us and the life you love best."

He had said very little; and yet the

words, sweetened by his manner and tone, sounded something like a promise. She was feeling just then so weak and spent that she drank in the tonic almost greedily, and brightened in a moment.

The afternoon mellowed into misty gold; velvety shadows rested on the grass, and even the leaves left off whispering and seemed to sleep in the universal calm. Godiva's misery had almost exhausted itself; it might gather new force and come back by-and-by; but just for a little while there was an interval of peace.

" Give me one smile," said Rex softly. " It is a poor little smile; but it will do if you have nothing better. Now, Godiva, don't you think you have exaggerated your troubles ? "

CHAPTER XIV.

FAREWELL LOOKS AND WORDS.

AMID much planning, sewing, and busy labour, Godiva's last days at Richmond flew away. She had resigned herself to her fate, and had even written a suitable and grateful letter to her uncle Hugh— a letter which Henrietta highly commended. And she had thankfully accepted the handsome outfit which the two old ladies had given her. It was good to feel that she was indebted to them for this kindness, and not to the uncle at Silversea. After a brief struggle with herself and a quiet talk with the sisters, she felt that it was well to go to the Durleighs beautifully dressed, and provided with everything that a girl, taking a new position, would inevitably require.

"For father's sake I will try to win them all," she used to murmur to herself in those last days. "And I must let them see that his influence is still a living influence in my life. If I am haughty, or bad-tempered, or self-willed, they will blame his training for my faults, and that must never be. It may take a long, long time to prove to them what father really was; but I must do it, and my patience must hold out to the end."

It was this idea which helped her to endure the thought of coming changes; and it did more, for it consoled her in the deeply sorrowful hours that came to her when she was alone. It was not an aimless life that she was called upon to live, although it was not the life that she had always planned for herself. There were quiet moments, spent in her little room at daybreak, when she gathered strength for the days that lay before her, storing up love and trust and tender memories to subsist upon by-and-by.

At last there came a day when she felt strong enough to go and take a farewell of the old street where she had spent the happy years of her girlhood. Aunt Susanna was not living there now. The house became unendurable to her after her niece had left it, and the shadow of death seemed to linger in every room. She had accepted the post of house-keeper in a large house in a West-End street, and was beginning life again with the quiet courage that elderly single women often possess. Nobody knew anything about the convulsive tears she had shed for the dear motherless child whom she had loved so long. Susanna Hayward was as silent in her grief as she had ever been in her joy.

When Charlotte Kemple heard of Godiva's proposed visit to Buckingham Street she wanted to accompany her. But the girl was steadfastly purposed to go alone.

"I am afraid it won't be good for you, my dear," said Miss Charlotte, yielding the point reluctantly. "But as you will have it so, I will leave you to yourself. You will come to me at Barnard's Inn, and Rex will give us an early cup of tea."

It was now early in September, and the great tide of humanity pouring through the Strand seemed at first to deafen Godiva with its rush and roar. She had been shut up a long while in the quiet house, hardly ever straying beyond the old garden, dreamy with the still lights and shades of autumn; her head was still too weak and her heart too faint to bear this sad return to a noisy world.

A little timid, a little uncertain about her strength, she turned slowly down the steep incline of Savoy Street, and lingered, looking at the grey chapel in its peaceful garden. It was good to come here, for it was here that her father had found the friendless girl clinging to these iron railings, and had brought her home. That girl was now in a safe shelter, leading her quiet, useful life in peace. Many a stray sheep had been gathered into the folds of Refuges and Homes; and he who had gone about seeking the lost ones was now himself at rest.

At that moment there came a soft peal of the organ, and then of boyish voices bursting sweetly into a hymn. All her life afterwards Godiva recalled the autumn light on golden leaves and green grass, and the wave of music sweeping out through the chapel door. It was a moment of parting and sadness and strange peace. Lingering there a little longer, she glanced up at a window which overlooked the sanctuary and its garden. It was at that window that Charles Dickens sat and wrote his pleasant paper on the Savoy precinct, and the verdant spot that he had loved preserved its old freshness still.

Then (still afraid to trust herself in Buckingham Street) she strolled on to the People's Garden, on the Embankment. There were men and women sauntering about; children were playing, but they were quiet in their play, and a sweet calm seemed to have fallen every-where. A light mist was slowly rising from the river; all was fair and faintly coloured, and touched here and there with dim gold. The air was filled with the scent of mignonette, a perfume which does not, like that of the hyacinth, bring melancholy thoughts with it. To Godiva this odour seemed to carry a faint suggestion of cheerfulness.

She went on slowly until she came to a seat that was near the old Water-gate, and then her heart began to beat with swift emotion. In days gone by she had come here with her father; he had sat on this very bench by her side, lost in his own musings while she had been busy with her dreams. While his mind had been occupied with all the perplexities of the men and women of to-day, hers had wandered away to the people of the past. The full river surged up to the steps of Duke Steenie's Water-gate; Vandyke figures of nobles and ladies filled the stately barges, and stepped out gingerly on those grey stones; the favourite duke himself, with his stiff ruff, delicate features, and pointed chin, rose up before her eyes. Well, they were gone—gone to their own place—and where the palaces of the great lords used to stand, there were streets teeming with busy life; where their barges had floated there were gravelled paths for humble men and women to tread in their leisure hours; and under the grey shadow of the duke's Water-gate the children of the poor had met to play. Years had come and gone with their good times and bad times, but bringing slowly and surely the victory of the people over the proud ones of the earth.

But how is that victory won? Not by deeds of rapine and violence; not by such wild mobs as those who laid waste the old Savoy Palace of John of Gaunt, and left some of their number to perish miserably in his wine-cellars; but by the patient courage of men and women who forgot themselves, and lived for their brethren; and by the wisdom of the few who calmly set themselves against bigotry, cant, and misrule. Sitting there in the sober autumn light, Godiva could be thankful for the conquests of the old days, and hopeful for the new.

And as the sweet wind touched her face, like a kiss of peace, she remembered the good Fuller's words, spoken, perhaps, within the grey walls of the old Chapel Royal, Savoy. "Not as a vulture, but as a dove," he said, "the Holy Ghost came down from heaven." It was the

dove-like spirit that she must carry with
her to Silversea if the victory there was
to be gained.

She was quite calm now—her eyes
were no longer wet; and a woman in
shabby mourning, holding a baby in her
arms, ventured to draw a little nearer.
Godiva turned her head and looked at
her.

"Lizzy Hammond," she faltered, growing very pale. Then she put one hand
on her heart, and shivered from head to
foot. But still the woman crept nearer,
holding up her baby.

"Miss Durleigh," said Lizzy, trembling, "I hardly know whether you'll be
able to bear the sight of me. If you
can't, dear miss, only make a sign, and
I'll go away."

For some seconds Godiva could not
trust herself to answer; but she made

no sign, and the woman stood still and waited. The baby, pleased with the sweet air and sunshine, set up a little shrill crow.

There was something in the tiny voice that touched the latent desire of motherhood which lies deep in the heart of every true woman. If Godiva had felt any repugnance to speak to Lizzy, it was gone now. She looked up quietly, and although her lips quivered she could smile. Then she gave a slight start.

"Lizzy," she said hurriedly, "your cap! I did not notice it at first."

"I thought they would have told you, miss," Lizzy answered in a steady voice. "It was well that he was taken. God knows I've never been a hard woman, even when he's used me worst;—but I can't wish him back."

Godiva looked away for a moment;

she could not meet the widow's eyes. Her glance fell on a young couple,—evidently an artisan and his sweetheart,—stopping to admire the scarlet geraniums. Would that girl ever be called to pass through Lizzy's experience? Would that man darken and blight the lives that were nearest to his own?

"Sit down here, Lizzy," she said gently. "I want to hear all about it. I don't know why I have not heard; —perhaps they thought I could not bear it."

"Ah, miss, you've been ill,—very ill!" Lizzy looked anxiously into the girl's wan face. "Often and often I've longed to know how you were; but I didn't dare to go near your house. And when I went to the Refuge to fetch baby they couldn't tell me anything. When Dick was took off to prison, miss, I went straight for baby. I couldn't live without baby a minute longer."

She gave the child a hug and a kiss. He was a bright-eyed little fellow of eight or nine months, and his soft, round cheeks bore witness to care and good feeding. Godiva suddenly bent forward and kissed him too.

"Father was always so fond of children," she said. "And he was so anxious about this little one."

The courting couple, sauntering past, looked with passing pity at these two pale girls with a cheery baby between them.

Lizzy Hammond had once been pretty, with delicately cut features and a rose-tinted face; but now the face was a sickly white, and the cheeks hollow. And Godiva, with her bronze hair rippling under her black bonnet, looked touchingly young and sad.

"Tell me everything, Lizzy," she went on. "My illness has kept me in ignorance of many things which I ought to have known; and I had not courage enough to ask questions. They took—him—to prison, you say? Oh, don't be frightened, Lizzy; I am quite strong now!"

"You aren't strong yet, miss," said the widow, keeping back a sob. "But maybe it will do you no harm to hear all I can tell. Yes; they took Dick to prison, kicking and yelling like a demon, and he didn't know what he had done till he came to himself. And then——"

"Yes, Lizzy?"

"He was a long while before he came to himself. He'd drunk and drunk his senses clean away, and there was nothing left in him but passion and devilry. But at last he did come to, and then they told him. He never rallied again, miss; only asked whether he'd killed one of the children as well as—— "

Something seemed choking in Lizzy's throat. Godiva, white as marble, was calm.

"Did he die in prison, Lizzy?" she asked.

"Yes, miss. There was some sort of disease at work in him, and anyhow he couldn't have lived much longer. I never saw him again alive after that awful night. But they said he kept praying with all his might to be taken. And he bade them tell me to keep little Ted from the drink. He sent his love to me, and said I was to get away back to my friends if I could."

Lizzy hid her face behind the baby, and wiped away a few tears. At last Godiva spoke again.

" Have you anywhere to go to, Lizzy ? " she said.

" My old country home was broken up years ago, miss," the other answered sadly. " I married Dick against everybody's will, and when he turned out so bad, and we sank lower and lower, I just dropped writing to my people. There's only my brother Ned left now. He and I were always fond of each other, and I named my Ted after him. When Dick was dead I wrote to Ned, and sent the letter to the vicar of the old parish at home. But Ned had left the place, and gone to Northsea."

" Northsea ? " Godiva repeated. " I think that must be near Silversea."

" Yes, miss ; quite near. Ned settled there and married, and took to a nurseryman's business. His wife died a few months ago and left him with a baby girl; and he's asked me to bring my children, and come and take care of the child. 'Twill be like beginning a new life," said Lizzy, musingly.

"I, too, am going to begin a new life." Godiva laid her hand on the widow's arm with a kind touch. "We shall see each other sometimes. My uncle lives at Silversea, and it is arranged for me to live with him."

Lizzy dried her eyes, and looked at her in wonder.

"It seems too good to be true," she said. "And, miss, I can't think how you can be so kind as to bear the sight of me! If it hadn't been for me and all my wretched troubles, the best man in the world would be alive now. I could have forgiven Dick for spoiling my life, but I never can forgive him for robbing the poor of their best friend."

" I hope God forgave him," said Godiva, with a very sweet look in her steadfast eyes. "Lizzy, instead of sundering us, this great sorrow ought to bring us nearer together. Father did not count his life dear; he was resolved to save your children at all costs, and he *has* saved them. His intention was to get the little ones out of their father's way, and then see what could be done with Dick. But that night—— "

Lizzy held up a thin hand in entreaty.

"Oh, stop, miss," she said; "you'll never know what that night was to me. I shall carry the wounds that he gave me to my dying day. Why need we go over it? Every day you may read a story just as sickening in the police news. He'd well-nigh done for me before your father came."

" Then we will not talk about it any

more." Godiva spoke with wonderful calmness. "Lizzy, I am going next week, and I will write to you if you will let me have your address. Now I shall take a farewell look at the river, and then at the old home."

Old Mike, the street porter, was standing at the corner of Buckingham Street, and one or two other shabby men came up to Godiva. She had a word for each of them. She did not lose her courage when they spoke of Morris; for his sake, and for those whom he had helped, she could bear anything. There was so much to say to the men, so many last things to tell them, that her good-bye to the old house was very brief. She noticed that the broad-leaved plants had been taken away from the window, and that there were new lace curtains smartly tied up with coloured sashes; and she

did not linger long at the familiar
door.

The men said many words about her
father that were good to hear. Such
words took the smart of pain out of her
heart, and filled it with great peace, and
" a solemn scorn of ills." Perhaps, in
all his hard-working life Morris had
never realized all that he had achieved
as his daughter was realizing it now.
He had sowed the good seed with labour
and pain, and his death seemed to have
forced it suddenly into flower and fruit.

Was the golden age nearer than she
had ever believed it to be ? To-day, in
spite of all her sorrow, it seemed very
near—the time that her father had prayed
and toiled for.

> " That Pentecost when utterance clear
>   To all men shall be given,
> When all shall say, *My Brother*, here,
>   And hear *My Son* in heaven ! "

CHAPTER XV.

IN A NEW WORLD.

TWILIGHT was coming on when Godiva joined Miss Charlotte at Barnard's Inn. Rex met her at the entrance of the narrow passage that leads to the Inn, and took care of her with grave kindness. His aunt was troubled at the sight of her pale face.

"It has been too much for you, my dear," Miss Charlotte said. "I tried to talk you out of your intention; but young folks are so self-willed. I was sure that no good would come of it!"

"Dear Miss Charlotte, good has come

of it," Godiva answered, " although it was harder even than I thought it would be."

She was so sweet and quiet that her voice thrilled Rex with sudden emotion. He put her gently into an easy-chair, and waited on her with silent tenderness. Tea was laid on Rex's round table; there was dainty brown bread and butter in an antique china plate; books were cleared away, and flowers were arranged in a pretty crystal vase. A small fire was burning in the grate, but the windows were open, and again the scent of mignonette came softly drifting across Godiva in her corner. If she looked at Rex, he did not return her glance, and yet she knew that he saw her plainly enough, and took care that she lacked nothing. Presently Miss Charlotte, having got over her brief vexation, began to talk.

"Bachelors know how to make themselves comfortable," she remarked. "I wonder whether Rex will fare any better when he is a married man?"

"My laundress came to ask if I was expecting two elderly ladies," he said. "She eyed the flowers with a suspicious air. I think she has a chronic objection to young women of every grade, and I don't believe she ever was a girl."

"But it wouldn't do, you know, to have a flighty young thing waiting on you," Miss Charlotte replied; "and very likely she would neglect your comforts. Yet I will say that your laundress is the worst mender of socks I ever saw. Godiva, you are eating nothing!"

Godiva smiled. Rex was standing with his elbow on the mantelpiece watching her quietly. Outside the windows golden leaves were dropping in the gathering dusk, and the air grew colder. Miss Charlotte rose to go.

"You are not going to Silversea till next Monday?" said Rex, as Godiva gave him her hand at parting.

"I am going on Thursday," she answered. "Did you not know? My uncle is coming to town on business, and will take me back with him."

He had not thought that the time of her departure was so near. Miss Charlotte, wishing to produce an effect at the last, had not told him. The old lady fancied herself a diplomatist, and walked off to the windows to smell the mignonette in the boxes. Rex was silent for a moment. He stood looking at Godiva, and a light seemed to come from his dark-blue eyes.

"This is not good-bye," he said in a low voice that thrilled clear and distinct through the little room. "I shall come to Silversea. Godiva, you will expect me after Christmas? You will not forget?"

She blushed up, and hesitated from sheer inability to express her pleasure.

"I shall be glad to look forward to something," she answered at last; "you know I shall be very lonely."

They did not say any more; and Rex conducted his visitors down the winding stairs, and out into the dusk. Godiva took a farewell glance at the plane trees shedding their gold into the quiet little quadrangle, and went forth into the noisy world to dream a girl's dream.

The last hours glided quietly away at Richmond. Godiva was very still, somehow; there were none of those outbursts of sorrow which the Kemples had dreaded. It was easy to see that she was weary with heartache; yet it seemed as if she could look away from the pain to some distant spot of sunshine and rest. It was that distant glimpse which made it possible for her to live her life just then; and she knew, long afterwards, that it is often this "devotion to something afar" which helps many a pilgrim over the roughest places in his journey. The "something afar" may turn out to be only a mirage after all—just a phantom paradise, made of chance lights and vapours—but not a few of us have been strengthened and heartened by such visions; ay, and have been led onward by them to a city "which hath foundations, whose builder and maker is God."

It was even harder to say good-bye to Joy than to the Kemples. Godiva always felt as if some mystical bond had existed between her father and the girl he had saved from want. She remembered how Joy's face had haunted him, and how he had found her with great rejoicing at last. And she loved Joy all the better for the sorrow that still lay like a cloud over her young life—the sorrow and yearning for her lost George and her lost faith in him.

Miss Charlotte went as far as Waterloo with Godiva and her luggage, and put her safely into her uncle's hands. There were last kisses, last promises to write very often; and then the train moved off, and Godiva found herself in the corner of a first-class carriage, face to face with Uncle Hugh.

It was not an unkindly face that confronted her, and there was, now and again, a fleeting look of Morris. But the eyes had not the peculiar steadfastness and clearness which had made

Morris's eyes so remarkable. Hugh
looked like a man whose life had been
fretted by small worries, although it had
never known one of those great sorrows
which confer a dignity on any life. He
had worked hard and looked to the main
chance, and had married a woman whose
money had helped him on in his pro-
fession; but somehow his home had
never been the resting-place that a tired
man needs. Honor and Janet and Sybil
loved him in their own fashion. They
were not troublesome girls, always crying out for more than he gave them;
and yet in his house he was vaguely
conscious of an atmosphere of discon-
tent. When he looked at Godiva, sitting opposite to him, with her pale
young face and quiet eyes, he wondered
a little at the peaceful expression that
she wore.

It was a dreary journey, although uncle and niece were honestly bent on getting on well together. He could not help wondering what would become of her if he were to die. While he lived he could give her a comfortable home, but he could not provide for her at his death; all that he had would belong to his children. Would she be likely to marry? He could not tell. In his eyes she seemed attractive, despite her paleness and fragility. His own girls were tall and large and fair—thoroughly Saxon, their friends said—and he scarcely thought that Godiva would be noticed when they were near. Yet who could say? This girl's delicate face, with the bright soul shining through it, might win the attention of some who would pass her cousins by.

It was evening when they reached

their journey's end. Mr. Durleigh was as kind as ever, but he could not be quite at ease when he thought of the ordeal that lay before him. Honor had said that she would, of course, receive her cousin with due courtesy; but Honor's notion of courtesy was intense frigidity. He knew that his girls did not like the intruder, and sooner or later they would make her feel this dislike. He was very sorry for their lack of cordiality; Morris had been the best brother in the world, and he wanted every one in his household to be good to Morris's child.

The mist was thickening every moment —lights were gleaming, vehicles coming and going, when they drove away from the railway-station. By-and-by a chill salt breeze came blowing into Godiva's face through the window of the cab.

"Uncle," she said, "are we near the sea ?"

"Yes," he answered, "and we shall be at home in a minute or two. I hope you will like the sea air, my dear; it ought to put new strength into you. Dear me, what a slow horse this is! Ah, well, here we are at last."

Godiva's heart seemed to give a great bound, and then stand still. It was a chilly evening, and she began to shiver from head to foot. When Mr. Durleigh helped her out of the cab he felt that she was trembling. He drew a deep breath of anxiety, and devoutly hoped that there would not be a scene.

The hall door opened. A stream of light flowed down the steps; a butler and a page presented themselves to Godiva's bewildered eyes. She did not know how she got into the hall, but had a grateful remembrance afterwards of her uncle's sustaining hold. They entered the drawing-room together; and some one who was playing on the piano stopped short.

"How do you do?" said Honor, in exactly the tone that Hugh Durleigh had expected of her. "It must be four years since we met. Are you very tired after your journey?"

Godiva tried to speak, and said something in a husky voice. A dry blast seemed to her to be beating about the house, choking her poor parched throat. They all thought her very stupid, she was sure. Her two younger cousins shook hands with her almost in silence.

"Perhaps you would like to go to your room," Honor continued. "We dine at half-past six to-night; our usual time is seven, but we are going to a concert. Don't trouble to dress. I am sure you are too tired."

They were all very much dressed; their gowns were black, it is true, but there was nothing sombre about them save the colour. Such a glitter of jet ornaments on arms and bosoms, and such a beady twinkling among their draperies! Godiva was thankful for the permission to retire, even for a little while, and collect her scattered thoughts. Her face looked so pale and frightened that they believed she was overwhelmed by their splendour.

Slowly, and with tottering steps, she followed a housemaid upstairs, and found that she was being taken to the top of the house. It was a small room which had been allotted to her, not too luxuriously furnished, although no necessaries were wanting. But that which struck the girl painfully was the utter lack of any little embellishment. It had not occurred to any one to hang up a picture or a wall-pocket, or even to put a pretty pin-cushion on the dressing-table. Godiva recalled the quaint decorations of her little room at Richmond; Miss Charlotte's dainty muslin flounces and frills, and the roses on ewer and basin; and never did simple love and kindliness seem so precious to her as now. Her new bedroom seemed to say plainly enough, "You are not wanted here; we will give you nothing more than the things you cannot do without. You shall have a shelter for your head, but it shall be a shelter unadorned with any token of goodwill."

When she had laid aside out-of-door garments, and had made a feeble attempt at smoothing her soft, rough hair, she felt very forlorn indeed. The glass reflected a pale face with two black marks under the eyes; the black gown with its crape folds looked heavy and plain; and the girls downstairs were waiting to criticize her. Here was a cheerful beginning of her first evening! She glanced at the narrow white bed in the corner, and wondered how many miserable nights she was destined to spend in it.

Her head ached, her heart ached; one loving word would have made the world a different place. She was glad to be alone, even in this bare little room, but she dared not indulge long in solitude. And then, quite suddenly and inconsequently, she began to look back on a bygone summer day when she had been with her father in the People's Garden. The bare walls were gone; there were the shrubs and flowers; the couples walking, the children playing, and the sun shining on the grey stonework of the old Water-gate. As she thought of all this her father's image came before her so vividly that she almost stretched out her arms. It was only an instant's impression, but when it had passed away she felt as if he had been really with her. All her resolutions to be strong and wise for his sake came back to her with renewed force. She must go downstairs and face them all, and live with them calmly and peaceably as he would have her live. It would not be easy, perhaps, but it must be done.

Tired as she was, it seemed a long journey down to the drawing-room where they were all awaiting her. The three girls scanned her with rapid glances, and then they went in to dinner in solemn

procession. Godiva tried to be hungry,
and tried to be grateful for the good
things set before her ; but gratitude had
come more readily at Garden Lodge
when Miss Charlotte had hovered round
her meals with all sorts of tender in-
junctions ; and Miss Henrietta had cooed
over her. Still, there are times in all
our lives when we have to do without
the presence of love ; and these times
are lived through with a fortitude which
often makes us wonder at ourselves.

"Are you fond of music ? " said Honor,
addressing her cousin in a chilly, affable
way. "I suppose you went to concerts
very often in town ? "

"We seldom went," Godiva answered.
"But—yes—I am fond of music. I like
to hear good singing."

"Then Janet must sing to you," said
Hugh Durleigh, with a glance of satis-

faction at his second daughter. "She is worth hearing."

"Godiva will soon hear enough of her," remarked Sybil, who was out of temper.

Godiva looked at Janet, whose face crimsoned with anger; and then she noticed that this second girl had a troubled expression about the brow and eyes. It was a stormy face that never looked at rest even when the features were in repose; a face that stirred up a vague sense of pity in Godiva's heart, and softened her voice (always gentle) when she spoke.

"I shall look forward to Janet's singing," she said, with a smile.

The smile was not returned. Honor came forward promptly with some trivial question, and Uncle Hugh helped her to make conversation with praiseworthy persistence. But there was a look of relief on his face when they rose from the table.

Of the three girls Janet was the plainest. All three were tall, and somewhat heavily made ; all three had light-blue eyes, complexions freshly pink and white, and plenty of fair hair, which was neither flaxen nor golden. Honor at two and twenty was good-looking, almost handsome perhaps, but too stiff and formal for her years. Janet was not so stiff, but more clumsy; and Sybil, who had the brightest face, could sometimes look malicious.

"Mrs. Steene always goes out with us," said Honor, putting on a furred cloak. "She is a charming woman, Godiva—our next-door neighbour. Of course, you won't stay up till we return. Good night."

They went their way, and Godiva did not linger in the empty drawing-room. She toiled wearily upstairs, and shut herself into her little room with a consciousness that it would, ere long, become a haven of rest; and then, mindful of Miss Charlotte's counsel, she went early to sleep.

 END OF VOL. I.

LONDON: PRINTED BY WILLIAM CLOWES AND SONS, LIMITED,
STAMFORD STREET AND CHARING CROSS.